---------------- ★ ----------------

OVER HER DEAD BODY

"I've got some exciting news to tell you. Me and Frisco here's going to get married." He held up her hand to show them the tiny diamond solitaire on the ring finger. Frisco simpered. Everyone else in the bar—not excepting Josh Leighland, the landlord—was dumbstruck. Dot was the first to recover the use of her voice.

"Over my dead body you will, boy!" She had him by the arm and was marching him out of the door before anyone else could move a muscle. Frisco, quite undaunted by the scene, remained in the bar, still looking smug. She gave Alison one of her lazy smiles and winked at her. Alison gave her a sharp look which Nick could not interpret. From the street Dot's voice could still be heard raised in anger, drowning the soothing mumblings of her eldest son.

"Over my dead body!"

---------------- ★ ----------------

" . . . much wryly civilized dialogue, sharp insights into village life, and a neatly turned puzzle provide a crisply entertaining second adventure for Inspector Trevellyan . . ."
—*Kirkus Reviews*

Also available from Worldwide Mystery by
SUSAN B. KELLY

HOPE AGAINST HOPE

SUSAN B. KELLY

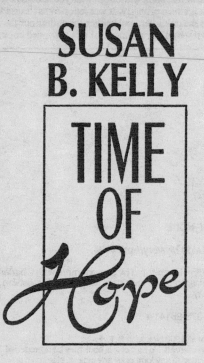

TIME OF Hope

TORONTO • NEW YORK • LONDON
AMSTERDAM • PARIS • SYDNEY • HAMBURG
STOCKHOLM • ATHENS • TOKYO • MILAN
MADRID • WARSAW • BUDAPEST • AUCKLAND

TIME OF HOPE

A Worldwide Mystery/April 1994

This edition is reprinted by arrangement with Charles Scribner's Sons, an imprint of Macmillan Publishing Company.

ISBN 0-373-26141-1

For Francis Clarke with abiding love

We shall not cease from exploration...

ONE

NICK PULLED HIS CAR into the courtyard of Hope Cottage at two o'clock on Tuesday afternoon. It was good to be home and spring seemed to have arrived at last during his absence. The flower beds which edged the gravel courtyard, still bare earth at the time of his departure, now displayed purple and white crocuses and the proud yellow trumpets of daffodils—all so late this year after the murderous snows of January.

He drew to a halt in front of the porch, got out and looked up at the silent house. No smoke was coming from the chimneys, nor was there any sign of Alison's car. Perhaps he had hurried back in vain.

He tried the old stable workshop first but found the door locked. The house door, surprisingly, was not locked and he pushed it open and went into the cool, oak-panelled hallway which smelt female—beeswax and lavender—in pleasing contrast to the beery, masculine environment of the police training college. It was a smell he had come to associate with Alison. It was a smell of order and grace and harmony.

He heard movement in the kitchen.

'Hello?' he called experimentally.

'Oh, it's you, Mr Trevellyan.' Dot Lawson appeared at the kitchen door, looking relieved. 'I thought we'd got a burglar for a minute.' She waved her mop menacingly to demonstrate that the burglar would have come off worse in the encounter, her strong red hands gripping the handle as she stabbed it in the air like a pike.

'Hello, Dot,' Nick said in surprise. 'Since when do you work afternoons?'

'It's just for today.'

'Where's Alison?' he asked. 'Upstairs?' he added hopefully.

'She went out after lunch.' Dot laughed at his dejection. 'She said she'd be back by tea time. You'll survive. She wasn't expecting you home before then, anyway.'

'No, that was what I told her. I got off a bit early.' He might as well have not braved the disapproval of his peers by dodging the final lunch and the maudlin farewells in the bar which always followed.

'She said something about the last box of six-inch floppies were duds and she'd have to get some more, only God knew where she'd find any. And if that makes sense to you then you're a better man than I am.'

'Computer discs,' Nick said, with more confidence than he felt.

'Shall I make you a cup of tea? I was just going to put the kettle on.'

'No thanks. If Alison's not here I think I'll go for a walk, blow the cobwebs away.'

'First dry day we've had for a week. It's blowy up on the moors, though.'

'Good. I'll just go up and change.'

He started up the stairs but Dot came trailing along the hall and called up, 'Mr Trevellyan, I've been meaning to say—Sam's getting home tomorrow.'

Nick stopped at the half landing and leant over the banister, looking down at her. She was a formidable sight, this *mater familias*, resting negligently on her mop at the foot of the stairs; her charlady's apron-and-slipper uniform only a partial disguise for her true nature which betrayed itself in every glance of her steel-blue eyes and every rigid lock of her gunmetal hair.

'That's good news,' he said sincerely. 'That's really great.'

'Yeah.' She gave him one of her rare smiles. 'Not that he doesn't get under my feet but I quite like having him around.'

'You make sure he stays out this time,' Nick said. 'He's getting too long in the tooth to go clambering up people's drainpipes.'

'That's right,' Dot said indignantly. 'There's younger blokes coming up, laughing at him—calling him granddad. No respect.' She managed to make Sam sound like a middle manager in ICI, constantly looking over his shoulder for the whizz-kid on the rung below, knowing that he's reached his own level of incompetence.

'It's not as if he's ever been any good at it, Dot,' Nick said gently. Sam's level of incompetence was the bottom level of the ladder.

'I know,' Dot said with dignity. 'You don't have to tell me. I went to see him about two weeks ago and he said this time was definitely the last. Now, I know he's said that before but I think he really means it. He says prison's not what it was—he doesn't feel at home there any more. It's what I say about the youngsters, you see, no respect for the old hands.'

She sighed and began to polish the newel post absentmindedly. Nick shuddered inwardly at the notion of a prison where even Sam Lawson, who'd spent two-thirds of his life there, didn't feel at home.

'He is getting on a bit,' Dot said thoughtfully. 'If only he could get some sort of job but I don't hold out much hope of that, things being what they are. He's got no skills except housebreaking. And, like you say,' she conceded, 'he's not much good at that.'

'How's he getting home?'

'Oh, Alan said he'd take me to pick him up, it being school holidays.'

'That's good.'

'He's a bit ashamed of him, of course, so it was nice of him to offer. I bet his snooty wife wasn't keen. She stops him coming over here to see me, you know.' Privately Nick thought that if he wanted to see his mother, Alan Lawson should be quite capable of standing up to his wife. But he could see no mileage in saying so.

'Your boys are a credit to you, Dot,' was what he said instead.

'You off on this holiday soon then?'

'Thursday afternoon. Back on Easter Monday.'

'Abroad, isn't it?'

'Italy. Venice.'

'Abroad,' repeated Dot, whose personal map of the universe had "Here Be Dragons" inscribed anywhere beyond Bristol. 'Nasty, smelly place by all accounts. All them canals. Damp. Unhealthy.'

'It's a point of view,' Nick said with a smile.

'And that olive oil in the food. It's not good for you.'

'We'll be careful,' he promised solemnly. He did not add that an overdose of chianti was a more likely threat to Alison's insides.

'Well, I'll let you get off on your walk,' she said briskly. 'Can't stand here gossiping all day.' As if it were Nick's fault. 'Got tomorrow's work to do today.'

'If I hear of anything that might suit Sam, I'll let you know,' he called after her. 'I might even be prepared to put in a good word for him if—and only if—he can convince me he won't let me down.'

'You're a good man, Mr Trevellyan,' Dot said simply. 'I've told Alison so a dozen times too.'

Nick laughed to himself as he carried on up the stairs to the bedroom. Goodness didn't cut much ice with his hard-headed lover.

NICK REACHED THE TOP of Threeoaks Hill half an hour later and pulled his ancient Ford to a halt in the least muddy patch he could find. He got out, stretched, and breathed in the clear, crisp air. To his west the moors streamed away flat for miles, while to his east lay the Hop Valley.

He changed into his scruffiest shoes and took his binoculars from the boot where he kept them, out of sight, after an embarrassing incident when his previous pair had been stolen from the rear seat. One of the uniformed inspectors had treated him to a lecture on crime prevention to the considerable mirth of the rest of CID. He trained the binoculars down into the valley and on to the village of Little Hopford.

Nick had known this valley all his life and the village itself held little interest for him. He focused his glasses instead on the house which he had come over the last nine months to call his home: Hope Cottage, separated from the rest of the village by three hundred yards of road and a tiny wood. Built of the local pink stone sometime in the eighteenth century, Hope Cottage was not a picture-book country cottage. Indeed, it was not a cottage at all but a substantial detached house with an acre of garden and a small paddock.

Nick had been delving into the history of the place during the long winter. It had been built by Sir James Gordon, baronet and autocrat, to keep a cadet branch of the family within reach of his whims. The Gordons had died out, their manor house institutionalised into a prep school, but Hop Cottage had survived—corrupted as Hope Cottage—which name had first drawn it to the attention of Alison Hope about a year earlier. Sick of London and looking to move her computer software business to the West Country, she had looked no further. She had bought Hope Cottage and crashed, almost literally, into Nick's life, sending him reeling.

He told himself that he had come to walk, not to spy on Little Hopford, although his earlier enthusiasm for the cold April day had shrivelled in the headwind of reality. He slung his binoculars over his shoulder and began walking resolutely towards the copse about two hundred yards away. He had hopes of seeing some red deer although it was not the best time of day. In two months there would be baby deer and he would drag Alison up here, by fair means or foul, to see if their frail beauty could touch her unsentimental heart.

The only other person in view was an elderly man whom Nick knew by sight but not by name; accompanied, as always, by a geriatric greyhound. The old man had grown spare and rangy like his companion— a long-standing couple this.

A rabbit bounded up a nearby bank and the greyhound's gaze followed it wistfully, its essential dogginess affronted by the creature's insolence. For a second it considered giving chase but finally accepted, with canine angst, that its rabbit-chasing days were over. It went to investigate a heap of litter instead. It squatted and staked out the litter pile for its own—determined to salvage something from the afternoon.

As their paths crossed, the old man caught Nick's eye and smiled. He did not speak. Nick did not remember ever hearing him speak. He felt a sudden urge for human communication.

'Good walking weather,' he said, wondering if that was really the best he could manage by way of communication. The old man did not think much of it, even as an opening gambit, since he merely nodded, glanced up at the racing clouds and walked on.

Nick plodded along, not paying much attention to the scenery. He was looking forward to a few days alone with Alison in Venice. She had been working flat-out since New Year on one of her lucrative computer games, but Nick got the impression that the game was nearly finished and in Venice they would be out of reach of her buzzing, flashing, headache-provoking computer terminals. He smiled.

Then he remembered Ben Lawson and the smile gave way to a frown as he vented his resentment on a pile of dead twigs in his path. Dot's youngest son hero-worshipped Alison and had begged to be allowed to spend his spare time sitting at her feet, metaphorically, and learning the business. Despite several months of cohabitation with Alison, the mysteries of her craft remained closed to Nick and he felt excluded. Ben was to study computing at Manchester Polytechnic in the autumn and Nick, who secretly doubted the existence of Manchester, hoped fervently that he would never be seen again. In the meantime there had been few evenings lately when Ben had not been hanging round the house or the stables.

Nick scowled so fiercely that the teenage girl who had just come out of the copse and was heading along the path towards him gave him a startled look. He composed his features and smiled at her. She recognised him and stopped, pleased to see him.

'Hello, Nick. You bin away?' She had the pleasing drawl of the unhurriable West Country.

'Just for a few days,' he agreed.

'Reckon Alison'll be glad to have you back.' She giggled then gave him one her broad, lazy smiles. 'Look what I've found.' She held up a hideous fungus which he didn't recognise.

'Whatever is it?' he asked, interested.

'Beef-steak fungus they call it, 'cause that's what it looks like, see.'

'Not edible is it?'

'Oh yeah. Want some?'

'No thanks,' he said with a shudder.

'It's good.' She nibbled the edge of the monstrosity experimentally, looking, for a moment, like Alice in Wonderland. 'See you,' she said, characteristically losing interest in the conversation, and bounced off back towards the valley, her brown hair floating in the wind. Nick wondered what or who she had been up to in the copse. Surely the ground was still too muddy even for Frisco?

He reached the stile which led into the copse and turned back to look over the moors. Frisco was still in sight. From this distance she looked much like any other teenager in jeans, anorak and trainers. She skipped over the ground, avoiding holes and mud patches with the skill of a moorland pony. As he watched, she rounded his car and disappeared down the steep hill path.

Nick slowly climbed the stile and began to trudge through the dense copse; the ground was slippery with last autumn's leaves, now well mouldered, and he had to watch his step. Overhead the clouds were rushing through the sky at an unnatural pace as the wind freshened. He wound his scarf a little more tightly round his neck and shivered.

TWO

NICK WALKED FURTHER than he had intended and it was past four o'clock by the time he turned his car into the courtyard of Hope Cottage once more. He felt pleasantly self-satisfied with his exertions, and more than ready to thaw out in sympathetic company. As he parked, the sun emerged from behind a cloud and the pink stone glowed its welcome in the filtered spring sunshine—its colour changing, as ever, according to the quality of the light: blood-red at midsummer twilight; clear grey as it reflected the snow.

A gravel drive led on from the courtyard between house and stable to a distant tumbledown garage. Standing on the gravel in front of the garage was Alison's black Jaguar convertible—its twin headlamps glaring at Nick's battered Ford with contempt. There were two things to be said in favour of the Jaguar: it wasn't a Porsche and it didn't have personalised numberplates. Nick made a face at it.

There was still no smoke coming from the chimneys, so he decided to try the workshop again. He pushed open the old stable door—with its inner door of plate steel designed to be both weatherproof and intruder-proof—and called a tentative greeting. Alison was alone. She was sitting at one of the VDUs gazing intently at the screen with something like disbelief. She glanced up when he came in, smiled vaguely, and resumed her staring. All she said was: 'Nick. Good.'

Alison was a single-minded young woman and believed in giving her full attention to whatever she was doing at the time, so Nick knew that extravagant displays of affection would not be welcome. He contented himself with putting his hands on her shoulders and kissing the top of her head. She picked up one of his hands and squeezed it without, however, taking her eyes from the screen.

'We've done it,' she said. 'It's finished. I can hardly believe it.'

"It" was an adventure game based on the cases of Hercule Poirot—the point of which evaded Nick. But he was mildly impressed by the enormous numbers of advance orders received for the game. He nuzzled her neck absently while looking at the screen. It showed a rotund, moustachioed Poirot clutching a vegetable marrow and wearing patent-leather shoes with impossible points. When Alison pressed a key Poirot walked aimlessly across the screen.

'It's the most complicated game we've ever done,' she said. 'I thought it was never going to work out. Christ, those graphics! I see them in my sleep.'

Nick glanced round the room wondering if Ben Lawson was going to appear suddenly from behind a printer or disc drive.

'No Ben?' he asked finally.

Alison groaned. 'I haven't seen him all week and apparently Dot hardly has either. She says he's got himself mixed up with Frisco. She's working herself up into a state about it and it's very heavy on the china.'

Alison wheeled back her chair, rose and stretched herself, rubbing at her shoulders where she had been hunched over her terminal. Nick gazed at her with admiration and love, finding it hard, as so often, to be-

lieve his luck. She was a tall woman, big-boned though
slender. The shower of red hair, which reached almost
to her waist when loose, was knotted neatly out of the
way at the back of her head. Her clear green eyes read
his expression with shrewd amusement. She was not
beautiful exactly—her features were too strongly de-
fined, her Roman nose too long for that—but sleek and
handsome and tawny like the lion whose mane she had
borrowed.

She was elegant, as ever, in a black cashmere jersey
and a kilt in what she liked to claim was her mother's
family tartan. Nick suspected, but could not prove,
that she wore it only because it was predominantly
black and green—the colours which most flattered her.
He put his arms round her, only half listening as she
continued with her story. After more than a week apart
his mind was on other things than Frisco and Ben.

It seemed that during one of her irregular visits to
tend the garden, Frisco had got into conversation with
Ben. Alison had thought nothing of it but Dot said that
Ben had been meeting Frisco in the evenings and visiting her in her cottage. Alison finished the story with
a shrug of her shoulders. Ben was eighteen. It was nat-
ural that he should want some experience of women
before he went off to college. Who better than the
willing Frisco? said the shrug.

'All girls round here think of nowadays is marriage
and three piece suites,' said Alison, secure in her substantial bank balance. 'The new morality. It's not like
in our day when people just went to bed together when
they felt like it.'

'Not round here they didn't,' Nick corrected. 'Frisco
had better be careful. Ben's the baby of the family and

young for his age, if you ask me. Look at the way he worships you,' he added spitefully.

'You worship me,' she pointed out.

'That's different. I'm not half your age. Besides I'm your... official... lover.' He gave her a long kiss—exhibit A in the evidence for this assertion.

Alison changed the subject impatiently. Ben and Frisco would work out their own affairs, they were both of age. It wasn't anyone else's business, not hers not Dot's. She motioned to Nick to take her place at the terminal while she went off to collect some listings from the printer. Gingerly he sat down and contemplated the screen.

'Just keep hitting "SEND" until the game really starts,' called the muffled voice from behind the printer.

Nick pressed the key, read the page of instructions which came up on the screen, pressed again and began experimenting with various commands as he had seen Alison do in the past. Computers, like Forster's memsahibs, seemed to know only the imperative forms of verbs. He tried "WALK EAST" and was gratified to see Poirot set off across the screen. A minute later he gave a cry of disgust as the fat Belgian was killed off by a passing psychopath. He restarted only to meet a similar end a little further into the game.

'It's so frustrating,' he complained. 'Um ... I'll just have one more go.'

'Actually you could be of some help to me in the instruction manual,' Alison said, returning with an armful of computer printout. 'One needs the layman's view to know how to pitch it.' She sighed, from which Nick gathered that the interesting part of the project was over and only the paperwork remained. He knew just how she felt.

She ran a hand through his tousled hair. 'You look as if you've been dragged through a hedge backwards. What have you been doing?'

'Just a breath of fresh air on Threeoaks Hill.'

'Go in and light the fire and put the kettle on,' said Alison who also favoured the imperative mood. 'I've just got to take some back-up copies of this and lock up. There are some crumpets in the kitchen.'

'Yes, ma'am.' Nick, who had just met with yet another gruesome end, gave up the struggle.

He let himself into the house. The fire was already laid and he put a match to it, watching with satisfaction as the little tent of twigs and kindling began to burn steadily until he was able to add some larger logs. He went into the kitchen, put the kettle on to boil and found the crumpets and toasting fork.

He heard Alison come in and go upstairs to her study where she kept her discs in the safe. He took the tray into the drawing room and set it down, pulling a soft leather Chesterfield a little nearer to the now lively fire. He lobbed a couple of fir cones into the back of the blaze for the pleasure of hearing them spit.

He smiled to himself as he watched the flames sizzling up the chimney. When Alison came in, he was practising a few Italian phrases under his breath.

'*Bella Signorina, donna bellissima,*' he said, seeing her. He patted the sofa and lapsed into English. 'Come and sit here, by me.'

'In a minute.' Alison poured herself a cup of tea and stood looking out through the french windows at the terrace. She was experiencing that slight strangeness which always followed a separation, however brief. The man on the sofa—her companion and closest friend; her lover—was for the moment an alien being.

Nick observed her at his leisure, silhouetted as she was by the fading south-westerly sun. Thus had she appeared to him on their first acquaintance: in the searchlight of events, yes, but unfathomable, hidden, private. The desperate passion he had conceived for her the previous summer had deepened over the colder months to embrace friendship and respect as he grew to understand and love her quick wits, her razor mind, her unpredictable moments of tenderness. She enthralled him. Hers was a character which needed a lifetime's study.

'Start toasting the crumpets,' she said, turning back into the room. 'I'll have two—no, three.'

'You are greedy.'

'I didn't have any lunch,' she said automatically. Then added in surprise, 'God, no, I didn't either.'

'Nor did I,' he countered. 'Which reminds me—have you made arrangements about dinner?' She shook her head. 'Only I thought we might go out to Hopwood Manor if you'd like.'

Alison didn't need much thinking time. ''Mmm, I would like to go to Hopwood.' There was always a sense of anticlimax at the end of a project. Really decent food and wine was just what she needed.

'We'll take my car,' Nick said. Alison made no objection, since he never allowed her to drink and drive and she was in the mood for drinking.

She sat down next to him on the sofa at last and laid her head on his shoulder. He put his arm round her and kissed the tip of her nose gently. She looked up at him, examining his well-known features anew: tousled black hair; watchful brown eyes; thin, bespectacled face.

Good-looking in an unobvious way, he would not have stood out in a crowd. His nature, so different from her own impulsive temperament, was mild and tolerant and thoughtful. The feeling of alienation went away in his familiar embrace and she realised how much she had missed him.

'I'm glad you're back,' she said. 'I missed you.' She stroked his cheek. He caught her hand and kissed it.

'*You* missed *me*!'

'Am I to infer,' she said solemnly, 'that you missed me, too?'

He kissed her nose again and then worked his way down to her mouth and then on to her neck, pulling the cashmere away from her shoulders. 'How lovely you are,' he whispered. 'You smell delicious. Mmm, you taste delicious too.'

'Is all this building up to an invitation to go upstairs, by any chance?' she asked pragmatically.

'Uh huh.'

'What are we waiting for then? I'll eat my crumpets later.'

THREE

MARGARET LOHITZUN-MENDI, who with her French-Basque husband Jean-Luc owned Hopwood Manor, was Nick's cousin. They were the same age and with Nick's young sister Gwen—always that bit smaller and slower—in tow, had spent their childhood leisure together. The Trevellyans were an unusually united family but Nick was not naturally gregarious and with his parents dead and Gwen permanently settled in Australia, Margaret was the only one to whom he had remained close.

'Before I forget,' Alison said, as they sped along the deserted valley road, 'Molly rang to invite us to a drinks party tomorrow night. I said we'd go.' Molly, Lady Armitage, was Alison's godmother and the nearest thing to family she had.

'Do we have to?' Nick asked misanthropically.

'I told her you had ten days' holiday due so I can't even claim that you've been called out.'

'What makes you think my being on holiday will stop them calling me out?'

'What? From Venice?'

'I don't think they'd go that far,' Nick agreed, 'But I'm keeping my head down until we're safely airborne.'

'But this party,' Alison insisted. 'Are you coming?'

'Of course I will.'

'Sophie's going to be there.' Nick looked blank. 'Molly and Anton's daughter.'

'Ah, the blue-stocking.'

'It'll be nice to see her again. She's so studious and vague.'

'It doesn't sound as if you have much in common.'

Alison smiled fondly. 'Dear Sophie is so impractical. Do you know, she can't even drive a car? I think she must bring out my protective instincts.'

'News to me that you've got any.'

'And the things she says! Anything she thinks, she just comes straight out with it.'

'I take it back. You have got something in common.'

'Huh! I can be charming when I want to.'

'I know you can. You have people eating out of your hand when it suits you.' *And spitting blood the rest of the time.*

'Don't talk about eating, I'm starving.'

'Alison, you can't possibly be. You ate *four* crumpets.'

'Well, I am. I can't wait to see what Jean-Luc's cooking up for us this time.'

The car park was half empty so early in the evening but Nick swung his car round the back of the hotel towards the tiny stone cottage which was the Lohitzun-Mendi's own home. He parked between the two square Renault 4s: the cheerful yellow one which was Jean-Luc's and the smart black one which was Margaret's.

'"Renault make a better car",' Alison read out. 'How come they keep selling people that one then?'

'It's a fun car. I used to have one when I was at Oxford—so old and rusty a strong wind would have taken it apart. I drove it all the way down to Rome one long vacation. Where's your spirit of adventure?'

'I can have adventures perfectly well in the Jag, and in comfort.'

He jumped out and held the passenger door open for her. As she got out, he hugged her tightly to him and said: 'I've missed you so much, my angel.'

She realised then that he was going to ask her to marry him that evening. She had thought that he would wait until they were in Venice—that city of lovers. A dark *calle*; a lugubrious canal; enough *strega*, and who knew what might happen?

MARGARET WAS PROWLING the dining room as Alison and Nick entered through the back door, gimlet-eyed for any breach in perfection. It was seven o'clock and she was making her final tour of inspection before the first diners arrived, her fingers lingering with pleasure on starched napery and sparkling crystal.

She was expecting them since Nick had telephoned earlier. Strictly speaking there hadn't been any free tables, but Margaret would always make room for Nick. She came forward to kiss them both. Privately she found Alison formidable—so tall and elegant and self-assured—but if she had had two heads and a tail, Margaret would have loved any woman who could put that elusive look of happiness into her cousin's eyes. She steered them both over to the bar but Nick refused a drink and went to pay his respects to Jean-Luc behind the green baize door.

'I hope Nick can cheer him up a bit,' Margaret said, as she mixed Kir for herself and Alison. She examined Alison out of the corner of her eye and decided that she was over-dressed in her flounced black taffeta. Like a fairy on top of the Christmas tree, she thought meanly, a wicked fairy in that black get-up. Spinning wheels and pricked fingers. How strange that Nick, who never gave his clothes a second's thought, should take up with this *Vogue* fashion plate. Surely this unlikely coupling would never last?

'Thank goodness spring is here at last,' she continued. 'Jean-Luc gets so depressed in the winter. Those four days in January, when we were snowed in, I thought he was going to go mad. As soon as it melted he was out running around like a man released from prison after twenty years.'

'It was rather claustrophobic,' Alison said. 'Nick said it was lucky all the villains were housebound too.'

'Nick says you're off to Venice. We don't seem to find time for holidays now. I don't know anyone I can trust to run the place in our absence.'

'You must delegate, Margaret,' Alison said sternly. She seated herself comfortably on a bar stool and looked at the older woman with sudden sympathy. Poor Cousin Margaret who was so large and plain and lumpen and who looked so harassed and weary. 'Or you'll wear yourself out.'

'I can't tell you how I look forward to Sunday evenings when we're closed.'

'Why do you open Sunday lunchtime? You could take the whole day off.'

'Jean-Luc likes Sunday lunchtimes—he wouldn't hear of our closing. In France it's a tradition for the whole family to go out for Sunday dinner—right down to the babe in arms. Family life is so important to the Basques.'

IT WAS ANOTHER WORLD behind the kitchen door where Jean-Luc and his slaves toiled in heat and noise like damned souls in hell. Jean-Luc, as large and as plain as his wife, embraced Nick with enthusiasm, almost crushing the breath out of him. Since Nick spoke French fluently they were able to carry on some sort of conversation despite Jean-Luc's basque accent and odd idioms.

Jean-Luc expounded at length on a new dish he had created involving snails in fennel sauce which he wanted Nick to try that very night. Since Nick didn't like snails he tried to change the subject, which got Jean-Luc on to talking about his wife. Business was good, he said, almost too good. All Marguerite seemed to do these days was lock herself away with the account books in that office of hers, emerging only to tell him how much they were now worth. They never took a holiday since she trusted no one with the hotel's reputation in their absence. What was it all for? Jean-Luc demanded of Nick. They couldn't take it with them. What was the good of a flourishing family business with no flourishing family? He picked up a meat cleaver and brought it down heavily on the worktop, frustrated by his inability to express himself adequately in words.

Nick, dismayed by Jean-Luc's uncharacteristic ill temper and at a loss for words of comfort, promised that Alison would sample the snails. That seemed to cheer him up and he allowed Nick to escape and rejoin the two women in the bar, where Margaret was eager to catch up on family gossip.

'Have you heard from Gwen lately?' she asked.

'Yes, just the other day.'

'I had a postcard from her in February. Surfer's Paradise, I think it was.'

'That's right. She took the children there for a whole month this summer. She's talking about coming over next year. She's dying to meet Alison.' Alison smiled politely. She was not dying to meet Gwen. Experience told her that no woman was ever good enough for big brother.

'Aunt Avis is coming to lunch on Sunday,' Margaret said.

Alison tried hard not to make a face. Of all Nick's large family, the loquacious Avis was the great irritant. Margaret caught the look and sighed.

'She is a bit of a trial. She's very lonely you know. Coming here for lunch occasionally is about the one treat she gets.'

'And a great treat it is too,' said Nick, who was anxious to get down to the serious business of the evening, which included eating.

'She seems such an unsuitable person to be the receptionist at the Health Centre,' Alison said. 'Surely discretion is the main qualification for something like that?'

'She inherited the job from Great Aunt Pansy Trevellyan,' Nick said seriously. 'It always goes to the oldest female of our branch of the family, isn't that right, Meg?' Margaret smiled wanly and Alison looked at him with suspicion.

'Knowing your family, I'm quite prepared to believe you.'

'Besides,' Nick said, tolerant as always, 'Avis is the safest kind of busybody to have in a job like that. Everyone knows she invents gossip if there's not enough of the genuine article about, so it follows that no one believes a word she says.'

Alison felt there was a flaw in his logic but was unable to put her finger on it.

THEY SAT DOWN to eat at about a quarter to eight. Nick held Alison's chair for her and was unnecessarily attentive all through the complicated business of ordering. She examined him covertly as he ate his fish soup in untypical silence: taking in his narrow wrists; the long, dark hairs of his forearms; the olive skin which tanned at the slightest hint of sun; his face—serious, almost melancholy, in repose. He was miles away, rehearsing his lines, but he must have felt her eyes on him since he looked up and smiled at her.

Nick had first proposed to her within weeks of their becoming lovers. He had accepted her early refusals with equanimity, saying that she was probably right and it was a bit soon, although that was not the reason she had given. Then had followed a period when her steadfast denials had caused him pain and been the occasion of arguments and bad feeling. Now he seemed reconciled to being turned down, which did not prevent the occasional resurgence of hope over experience. Alison wondered what approach he would choose tonight and hoped that he would have the good sense to wait until the coffee.

She picked her way through her snails—she didn't care for snails and was not at all clear how she had come to order them—and was well into her supreme of chicken with green peppercorn sauce, when Nick struck.

'The flat below mine is up for sale,' he began, and for a moment the proposal almost crept up on her unawares. 'I could think about putting mine on the market.' Alison said nothing, she wasn't going to help. 'I mean,' he went on, abandoning his fillet of English lamb with juniper to take her right hand in both of his, 'it's not as if I spend any time there, is it?'

Alison put another large forkful of chicken into her mouth with her left hand to make it clear that no comment was to be forthcoming. He tried again. 'If we were to get married—' She was shaking her head. 'Oh, well,' he said, without rancour, 'Some other time perhaps.'

'My accountant wouldn't stand for it,' was the only reply Alison made, as she reclaimed her hand and refilled her glass with best burgundy. 'You know, one of the things I like about this place is that you can fill your own glass up without fifteen waiters descending on you in a rugger scrum, all tut-tutting in unison.'

Nick smiled dutifully. She had made her usual answer to his proposals—he had not really expected anything else—and he was forced to acknowledge the truth of her assertion that the tax laws were not designed for the convenience of married women. Now she had changed the subject and the ground rules prevented him from re-opening it. But he was feeling peculiarly stubborn tonight.

'I love you, Alison,' he said. 'I've missed you like mad these last few days. Not just your beautiful, sleek body either. But the way you moan "God! What the hell time is it?" when my alarm goes off in the mornings; and the way you eat crumpets so the butter gets all over your chin and runs down your fingers—'

'There you are, you see,' she began incoherently.

'—and the way you talk with your mouth full.'

Alison swallowed her chicken. 'We're fine as we are. I don't believe in marriage.' She reached across and squeezed his fingers briefly. 'Eat your lamb. It's costing you enough.'

Jean-Luc appeared at that moment to ask what Alison had thought of the snails. Nick hastily assured him that she had found them perfectly delicious.

'*Chère Alisonne*,' Jean-Luc said, kissing his hand vaguely in her direction. '*Toujours si belle, si élégante*.' Alison smiled non-committally.

'What did he say?' she asked when he had gone. Alison belonged to the Speak Loudly And Clearly In English school of communication (More Loudly The Second Time If Necessary).

'He said you were a bit of all right,' Nick translated freely.

'Oh. It obviously sounds better in French. What's for pudding?'

They spent the rest of the meal squabbling amicably over what they would do in Venice. Alison vetoed too many hours spent in art galleries and churches in favour of gondola rides and more excursions into the lagoon. It was late when they set off back towards Little Hopford. The wind had dropped and it was a clear, frosty night. Nick drove more slowly than usual, enjoying the sight of the hills rising round them in the moonlight as they descended the valley.

'Sell your flat by all means,' Alison said, leaning back comfortably in her seat. 'Just because I don't want to get married, it doesn't mean it's not for keeps. Hope Cottage is your home too now.'

'I think I'll hang on to it for the time being. It's very convenient if I have a late night.' He glanced sideways at her. She had closed her eyes and was humming a little tune. She opened her eyes and saw him looking at her.

'Watch the road.' Nick watched the road. 'My Grandfather Hope was a lepidopterist,' she said unexpectedly. 'That's someone who collects butterflies.'

'I am familiar with the word, thank you, dear.'

'Oh. Well, when he wanted to add a butterfly to his collection he suffocated it in a jar first, then pinned it to a board. Dad's study at the vicarage was full of the horrid things. That's what marriage is like.'

'I would be a very liberal husband,' Nick said humbly. 'I wouldn't pin you to a board or chain you to the sink.'

Alison laughed and closed her eyes again and did not bother to reply.

FOUR

'THERE.' Nick stepped back from the grate the following morning and looked at his handiwork with pride. 'I'd have made a wonderful arsonist.'

'It's not too late,' Alison said. 'You know all the right people. Blast! I just remembered, Dot's not coming in today. Someone Else will have to tidy up.'

'Yes,' Nick said. 'I wonder who.'

'She said something about Alan taking her to pick her husband up. I didn't understand that. I haven't a clue who Alan is and I thought she was a widow.'

'No, old Sam Lawson is alive and kicking.'

'Then where's he getting back from?'

Nick knelt in front of the fire again and began to poke it vigorously. He felt safer with the poker in his hand. Alison did not consider violence to be a last resort—nor indeed a second-to-last resort.

'Um, the Scrubs this time, I think.'

'What! Prison? Is that what you're saying?' Nick nodded. 'Dot's husband is a jail bird?'

'Incorrigible.'

'Why the hell didn't you tell me? . . . Nick, leave that stupid fire alone and look at me.' He obeyed, observing her indignation with amusement. He felt like falling into an old film script and telling her she was beautiful when she was angry. But Alison probably didn't know her lines.

'Why didn't you tell me?' she repeated.

'Is Dot a good cleaning lady?' he asked, squatting on his heels and weighing the poker in his hand.

'You know she is.'

'You've found her hard-working and honest, haven't you? In fact you have made yourself extremely unpopular in the Hopfords by bribing her to do more hours here at the expense of her other employers. Right?'

' . . . Yes.'

'And would you have employed her if you'd known?'

'Well . . . probably not.'

'There you are, then. I've done you a good turn. Say "Thank you, Nick".'

'It would have been nice to have known. What does he go in for?'

'Burglary.'

'Nick!'

'It's all right, my angel. He wouldn't dream of burgling any of Dot's employers. In fact it's quite a worthwhile insurance policy.' Nick put down the poker and sat next to her on the sofa. 'Look, I've got a lot of time for Dot Lawson. Sam's been in and out of prison for the whole of their married life and she's brought up three kids on her own earnings and brought them up decently. I knew you would pay her well and I knew she was a good worker. So everyone is happy, right?'

'It explains something that puzzled me, anyway. When I went round to see her about the job, she asked if I lived alone in a tone of voice which implied that she knew all about my sinful ways. So I said no, Nick Trevellyan lived here too. Then she said did Mr Trevellyan know I'd come to see her. I said yes, in fact you'd recommended her. Then she looked relieved and said that was all right then. I didn't know what she meant but I see now she assumed that you'd told me.'

'I wonder how long old Sam will stay out this time,' Nick said. 'The old fool's so incompetent it's almost a shame to arrest him.'

He told her about the last time. Sam had broken into a house in Great Hopford. He'd been watching it for a few days—seeing the wife go off to pick the children up from school each day. So he chose a day, nipped in the kitchen window, and ran straight into the woman's father who had come for a short visit with his pedigree Rottweilers.

'We had to send a constable round to rescue him in double quick time,' Nick said, 'as the Wing Commander had his own views on suitable retribution. Then I got him to admit to three other burglaries in the area all of which yelled "Sam" to the practised eye. He never wants to admit to anything. He can't grasp that it's better for him that way: it means he wipes the slate clean.'

'And you improve your clear-up figures,' Alison said cynically.

'And he gets concurrent sentences. Three years that time—out in two. He's always a model prisoner.'

'Perhaps the Wingco had a point then,' Alison said, glancing round at her own much-treasured possessions.

'He's just so harmless that it seems a waste of society's indignation.'

'Odd Dot doesn't hold it against you, sticking her old man inside all the time. In fact, I think she has a soft spot for you.'

'She's very law-abiding. I think she'd be the first to say he deserves everything he gets.'

'You said three kids? She's never said she had any others. Other than Ben, I mean.'

'No? She's not the most garrulous of people, is she?'

'One of her best qualities, if you ask me.'

'There's Alan, he teaches at the comprehensive, he must be about thirty. Greg left university a couple of years ago and is training with a firm of accountants in Exeter. Then there's Ben.'

'Big gaps between them.'

'We haven't started allowing conjugal visits yet.'

'Oh . . . I see what you mean. I think I've met Alan Lawson, it didn't occur to me he was related to Dot. He's done quite well for himself.'

'He married the bank manager's daughter.'

'I didn't take to him, I must say, but it must be awfully embarrassing for him to have a father like that. Strange Dot's stuck by him all these years.'

'Mmm, Sam's not such a bad husband—when he's around. He was remanded in custody when they got married. They let him out for the ceremony. Dot was expecting Alan at the time—result of a bit of freelance getaway driving Sam had been doing up in Bristol. That's always been his trouble really—he's careless. Dot certainly gave the Lawsons a good shake up. She had old Mrs Lawson on a very tight rein by the end of the first week—made her springclean the house. First time in decades.'

THEY ARRIVED PUNCTUALLY at Lady Armitage's party. Molly, who had to stand up straight to reach five foot, balanced on tiptoe to kiss Alison's cheek as she stooped. She shook hands with Nick.

'I'm so glad you could come too, Nick.'

'It was nice of you to ask me, Lady Armitage.'

'Alison, Sophie is here at last.' Molly turned and yelled across the room: 'Sophie! Here's Alison and her Young Man.'

Dr Sophie Armitage was one of the least co-ordinated women Nick had ever seen. She managed to combine her mother's small stature with her father's gangling gait, making him fear for the safety of Molly's collection of Staffordshire dogs. But her pale face glowed at the sight of Alison and the two women embraced as long-lost sisters.

'I'm glad Molly did the introductions,' Alison said. 'I never know what to call Nick. "My Boyfriend" makes me sound about seventeen and "My Lover" makes me feel like Catherine the Great. "Young Man" is just the thing.'

Nick smiled at her affectionately. 'I think Sophie has got the message.' He turned to Sophie. 'You're a history don at Oxford, aren't you, Sophie?'

'Yes, Somerville.'

'I read one of your books,' Nick said. 'About the power structure of Renaissance Italy. I found it fascinating.'

'Alison!' Sophie said, 'I do like your "Young Man" enormously.'

'Sounds too dreary for words,' Alison said unkindly.

'You wouldn't believe Alison read history at Cambridge, would you, Nick?' Sophie said. This thought had often struck Nick. It wasn't just that Alison seemed to have forgotten it all but that she gave the impression of never having known it in the first place.

'Only in my spare time, though,' she said, enlightening them.

'I was riveted,' Nick went on. 'The Borgias; the Medicis—a fascinating study of power and corruption.'

'Yes, they make *Dallas* look like the *Archers*, don't they?' Sophie said. 'People talk about our era as if murder and fornication had just been invented. They should find out a bit about the fifteenth century.'

Alison perked up at the mention of murder and fornication. 'Nothing like a good murder,' she said. 'Keep the police on their toes.'

'I'm being frightfully tactless as always,' Sophie said. 'Mummy wrote and told me about your cousin, Alison, but I have to bring the subject up.'

'I don't mind at all. That was all ages ago, nearly a year.'

'But Mummy said you were under suspicion—that the local police inspector nearly arrested you.'

Alison squeezed Nick's arm. 'This is him.'

Sophie looked embarrassed. 'I can't believe it—that you're a policeman, I mean.'

'Exactly what I said when I first met him,' Alison said triumphantly. She glanced round. 'Oh look, here's Reg Grey. Will he acknowledge our existence, do you think?'

'Reg Grey?' Sophie peered short-sightedly across the room. 'He's the superintendent, isn't he? Is he your boss, Nick? Why shouldn't he acknowledge you?'

'Reg has his blind spots,' Nick said, 'and at the moment Alison and I occupy one of them.'

'I'm going to speak to him,' Alison said. 'I shall force him to admit I exist. Here, hold this.' She held out her gin and tonic to Sophie, thought better of it, handed it to Nick and set off across the room.

Nick made a face. 'Alison rushes in where angels fear to tread.'

'She always has,' Sophie said. 'You won't change her.'

'I don't want to. One of the things I love most about her is her vitality, her irrepressible spirits.' They turned to watch Alison advance on Reg Grey with outstretched hand. He had no choice but to take it. 'When things are blackest,' Nick said admiringly, 'and everyone else is sitting round moping, Alison is out there cracking jokes or picking a fight.'

'Usually the latter,' Sophie agreed.

Alison returned and reclaimed her glass.

'Happy now?' Nick asked. 'Been well and truly snubbed?'

'He couldn't snub me, not in front of Molly. He said, "Ah, Miss Hope Ummm."' She laughed. 'How long are you up here for, Sophie?'

'Just for Easter, then I'm going to Paris to look up some of the Medici archives there, then I'll be back for another day or two.'

'Well meet me for lunch one day when you get back.'

'Why can't Sophie come to dinner?' Nick suggested.

'I'd like that,' she said.

Alison got out her filofax. 'Then let's fix a date. When are you back?'

'Thursday and Friday a fortnight from now, I think. Yes that sounds about right. The . . . thirtieth?'

'Come on the Thursday then.'

'Perfect.'

Alison and Nick made their excuses and escaped on to Molly's balcony and looked out across the Channel.

'I suppose we could get a sailing boat,' Alison said.

'I suppose so. I don't know when I'd find time to sail it though.'

'I could sail it.'

Nick laughed. 'Ever sailed a boat?'

'Well . . . no.'

'There you are, then.'

'Have you?'

'Well . . . once, but the Trevellyans have lived on this coast since Time Immemorial—they were smugglers centuries ago. It's in the blood.'

'Huh! My ancestors have been vicars since Time Immemorial—doesn't mean I'm licensed to conduct weddings, christenings and funerals, though.'

Nick stamped on this woolly thinking at once: 'They can't have been.'

'What?'

'Vicars since Time Immemorial. Only since the Reformation.'

'Oh, fair enough. It's about as likely as your family being smugglers anyway.'

'Smugglers and wreckers,' he elucidated.

'A proud boast—for a policeman.'

'Well, it's Uncle Lynton's boast really.'

'Your Uncle Lynton is completely potty.'

'He is not. He owns an old smugglers' inn so he tells tales of old smugglers. It's good for business—a concept which you, of all people, must understand.'

IT WAS A PERFECT spring evening and after a late supper Nick suggested walking down to the village.

'We can have a nightcap at the Bird in Hand,' he said. Alison had cupboards full of nightcaps at Hope Cottage but she readily agreed to a moonlit stroll. They set off along the footpath which led from Hope Cottage, through the wood, to the village.

Nick stopped to tie his shoelace outside the pub so Alison went in first and was already ordering when he joined her. If Nick had been first he would probably have called a halt to the expedition. In the far corner of the bar sat three members of the Lawson family. Alison, turning with their drinks, spotted them too.

She looked with frank interest at the man sitting next to Dot. He wasn't at all what she had expected. She had had a mental image of a stereotyped old lag: undersized but flabby, weasel-faced. Instead Sam Lawson was a neat little middle-aged man with a fine head of white hair. A pair of bright blue eyes looked Alison up and down briefly and with approval. He caught her staring at him and winked at her. To her fury she felt herself blushing and looked away quickly.

The third member of the party she recognised as Alan Lawson, the schoolmaster. He was in the corner seat and occasionally looked round the bar nervously in case one of his smart friends from Hopbridge should appear and see him in such company.

Sam had his back to the door and if he had seen Nick he gave no sign of it. He was obviously the life and soul of the party. Dot was giggling tipsily and even Alan managed a smile from time to time.

Nick steered Alison over to the farthest corner and whispered, 'Let's make it a very quick one.' But Alison was not so sensitive. She caught Dot's eye and gave her a wave. Dot got up and went over to them.

'Evening, Alison, Mr Trevellyan.'

'Can I get you a drink, Dot,' Alison asked.

'No thank you, miss. I just wanted to ask if Ben had been round to you today.'

'No, I'm afraid not. I haven't heard a word from him for days.'

'Well, I just thought I'd ask. G'night, miss, sir.'

Dot went unsteadily back to her corner with a worried look. Nick drained his beer and cleared his throat.

'Well—'

The saloon bar door opened and in came the fugitive Ben, eighteen years old and the apple of his mother's eye, with Frisco Carstairs. He didn't notice Nick and Alison but went purposefully over to the other corner, holding Frisco by the hand. Frisco looked pleased with herself. Dot jumped up and confronted her son.

'Where the hell you bin, Ben Lawson? I bin looking for you all day. Fine time to go disappearing, with your dad just home, and not even let Miss Hope know where you'd got to.' Ben's gaze followed the pointing finger to where Alison was trying, unsuccessfully, to look as if she wasn't listening. Ben gave her a nod and a vague smile.

'I'm sorry if you were worried, Ma. I've got some exciting news to tell you. Me and Frisco here's going to get married.' He held up her hand to show them the tiny diamond solitaire on the ring finger. Frisco simpered. Everyone else in the bar—not excepting Jos Leighland, the landlord—was dumbstruck. Dot was the first to recover the use of her voice.

'Over my dead body you will, boy!' She had him by the arm and was marching him out of the door before anyone else could move a muscle. Sam and Alan, taken completely by surprise jumped up and ran after them, although Sam paused long enough to finish his pint. Frisco, quite undaunted by the scene, remained in the bar, still looking smug. She gave Alison one of her lazy smiles and winked at her. Alison gave her a sharp look which Nick could not interpret. From the street Dot's voice could still be heard raised in anger, drowning the soothing mumblings of her eldest son.

'Over my dead body!'

THE NIGHT IS NOT SILENT in the country. When the humans have followed their dogs home to the fireside, the night shift takes over in the copse on Threeoaks Hill. The wood mouse explores the murky compost of last year's leaves, pricking his ears occasionally against the barely audible whisper of the rounded wings of the tawny owl. The rat is king here—lord of the copse. Sometimes a fox or an adder deposes him, temporarily. He will be back with reinforcements.

Easter is very late this year and spring has followed its example. The copse is damp and joyless this Easter Sunday night. The human inhabitants of the valley do not venture much into Threeoaks Copse on the mildest of nights. It has . . . a reputation to keep up.

The figure which lies under the largest of the oaks is not afraid of its reputation—has probably never heard of it. But then the figure is not human.

Not now.

A Cockchafer beetle sprints, purposeful, through the straight fair hair on its way home. In the morning birds, concerned only with the next generation, will size it up as nest material. Its head, sidelong on the leaf mulch, has no expression, not even surprise. There was no time for that. Its eyes are open. Its mouth is also open since it gasped with such futility for breath a few minutes ago. It is not human for it has no voice. Its last words—'Zat you?'—will not appear in any history books.

The other figure has also abandoned any claims to humanity. It has an expression though: terror.

And a voice.

Not loud: more of a low, hopeless moan. It whimpers as a child whimpers, unable to accept the inevitable; certain that a little extra pleading can change the unchangeable. If only it can find the Open Sesame.

No. Please get up. Oh God. No.

Don't just stand there. Someone might come. Run.

The figure turns and runs, slithering on the wet leaves. The branches tear at its face, or so it seems. The roots reach for its feet, or so it seems. The one-time human who lies at the foot of the oak is not as friendless as you thought.

Get far away from here. Keep your head. Don't panic. Deny everything. Run. Keep running. Lie. Lie. Keep lying. You may be lucky.

IT WAS NOT Dot's dead body that was to prevent the alliance of the Lawson and Carstairs families.

Alison and Nick left for Venice the next day. On their return on Monday night, they learnt that the body of Frisco Carstairs had been found strangled in Threeoaks Copse that morning.

FIVE

'ALL I'M SAYING is that if you'd been polite to him, he would probably have let you off with a warning.' Nick took both suitcases out of the boot of the Jaguar. Alison unlocked the front door and switched off the burglar alarm.

'They should have better things to do than harass innocent motorists. My car's built for speed and I'm a very experienced driver. It's not people like me who cause accidents—it's the old dodderers doing fifty in the fast lane.'

'"If you're going to book me, get on with it. I'm in a hurry." I didn't know where to look.'

'I don't see why you couldn't have pulled rank on him. He was only a constable.'

'What! The Thames Valley police eat provincial detectives for elevenses.'

'They don't usually sneak up on me like that. I must be losing my grip.'

'Next time just smile sweetly,' Nick said, 'tell them you're very sorry and you'll never, ever do it again—and flash your legs at them, OK?'

'Oh, well,' she said, shrugging off her disgruntlement as easily as she shrugged off her jacket. 'I've been speeding for over ten years and this is only the third time I've been stopped.'

Nick began to laugh. Alison thought that not getting caught was the only point at issue. 'You'd better ask for ten thousand other offences to be taken into consideration then,' he told her.

'There are some messages on the machine. Let's have a look.'

'I'll take the suitcases up while you sort out the post and put the kettle on.'

He went upstairs. Two minutes later Alison called up to him. 'Nick! I think you'd better come down. Urgent message to ring Bill Deacon.'

DETECTIVE SERGEANT DEACON, Nick's deputy, was obviously very glad to see his boss, if apologetic at his early recall from leave.

'I'm afraid it's partly my fault, sir,' he said. 'I mentioned that you more or less lived at Little Hopford these days and the Super seemed to think—'

Nick brushed the apology aside. 'You couldn't leave me out of a murder on my own ground. Besides, I may be an eye-witness to an important bit of evidence.'

'What's that?'

'It can wait. Let's hear all the details first.'

Placid Bill seemed unusually agitated as he explained the events of that day. 'The body was found at about nine o'clock this morning by a woman, a lady, out walking her labrador in the copse.'

'What woman?'

'Mrs Swift from The Old Mill House in Great Hopford.'

'What! Penelope Swift?' Nick queried in dismay.

Alison, with her usual lack of moderation, had plunged headlong into local affairs since her arrival in the valley and had offered to "help" organise the Hopfords' traditional Whitsun fête which meant, of course, that she had completely taken over. Nick had noticed the vicar wandering around looking dazed as if Mephistopheles had just made him an offer he couldn't refuse. Mrs Colonel Swift, accustomed to ruling the roost, had taken to coming round to Hope Cottage and dripping honeyed venom all over the polished floors.

'That's the one,' Bill said. 'She said she was a friend of yours.' Nick made a rude noise and Bill smiled faintly. 'The body was out of sight in the thickest part of the copse but, of course, the dog sniffed it out. She didn't have hysterics, that Mrs Swift.'

'I imagine not.'

'It took her twenty minutes to get back down to the village and we had the place sealed off by quarter to ten. They've been over every inch of ground but the rotten leaves hadn't taken any footprints. And of course the dog had scrabbled about, moved things and so on.'

'How was it done?'

'Strangled, with her own scarf. Not a woolly muffler, some mauve and yellow flowered thing she had tied round her neck.'

'Sex murder?'

'Not clear at the moment. Doctor Brewster said there'd been intercourse but there was no bruising, so he reckoned it was done without any force being used.'

'Could have been done after she was dead, of course.'

'Christ! Do you have to?' Bill gave Nick a sour look.

'Sorry. Just thinking aloud.'

'He's doing the PM tomorrow morning. He estimated the time of death on the spot as middle of last night. Rigor was just about fully established when we got there—but it's damn cold at night at this time of the year. There's a young man in the village who claims to have been engaged to the girl.'

Nick nodded. 'Ben Lawson. I know all about that. You've had him in for questioning, of course?'

'I had him in all day but I let him go in the end. He says he was at home all yesterday evening and night with his mother and father and they back him up. Besides which either the poor kid is devastated or he's a budding Laurence Olivier. But she obviously had a bloke with her, some time that evening, and who would it be if not her intended?'

'Almost anyone I'm afraid, Bill. You didn't know Frisco.'

'Immoral?'

'No. Amoral.'

'. . . I see. You say you knew about the engagement, sir, but apparently it only happened on Wednesday.' Nick told him about the scene in the pub. Bill gave a low whistle. 'So old mother Lawson was dead set against it, was she?' Bill had not taken to Dot who had bullied him mercilessly in the protection of her chick. 'Dead set enough to be behind something like this?'

'If you mean do I think Dot Lawson got on her bicycle, enticed Frisco up to the copse with promises of a cosy mother-in-law-to-be chat and then strangled her, the answer's no. Anyway we know there was a man there at some time that evening. It's ninety-nine per cent certain that he was the killer. I shall have a talk with Ben myself, of course, but it can wait until I've had a look at the copse. Have the SOCOs finished there or will they be going back tomorrow?' Bill confirmed that the Scene of Crime Officers had finished.

'What about the rest of the gang?' Nick asked.

'Miss Halsgrove and Penruan are doing house-to-house in both the Hopfords. They'll carry on with that tomorrow.'

'Good.'

'Speaking of which.'

'Yes?'

'Penruan's annual report is due.'

'I know.'

'The papers are on your desk.'

'It can wait until this is all over.'

'The Super said A.S.A.P.'

'The Super can go and ... have a bit of patience.'

'He's slapdash and insubordinate,' Bill said.

'I know, but he is the Superintendent.'

'Penruan,' Bill said patiently. 'Not Mr Grey.'

'Youthful high spirits.'

'And promiscuous. That's always a security risk.'

'I think that's a bit unfair. There's no evidence that he discussed his work with girls. He's probably less of a security breach than you and I who have wives ... or whatever ... we confide in.'

'He's sly too, manipulative. He uses people.' Bill Deacon was the most easy-going of men but once he got his knife into someone, they needed surgery to remove it. 'My advice is to get rid of him, sir, while you've got the chance.'

'We'll see,' Nick said. 'Who would I play squash with?'

'Pah!' Bill said. 'Maybe someone you can beat occasionally?'

They parted at midnight and agreed to meet at Threeoaks Copse early the following morning.

Alison was asleep when Nick got back to Hope Cottage. She had left a note saying, "Wake me up before you go out in the morning. Urgent."

'WAKE UP, sleepy,' Nick said at seven o'clock the next morning, giving her a little shake. 'I've brought you up some tea.' He was already dressed and breakfasted.

'Ugh, when I said wake me up I didn't mean in the middle of the night,' she protested.

'Why did you want to be woken up, anyway?'

'To hear about Frisco, of course.' Nick frowned at this untypical ghoulishness but told her the brief facts as he knew them.

'I suppose the post-mortem will show whether she was really pregnant or not,' Alison said slyly.

Nick pulled her into a sitting position. 'Okay, you've achieved your dramatic effect. Applause. Now spill the beans.'

'She told me about a week ago. She was doing the garden one day and came into the workshop to find me. She waited until Ben wasn't there. She said she was late and I told her she had to go to the doctor. In fact I rang up and made an appointment for her, then and there.'

'And did she tell you who the father was?' Nick asked eagerly.

'I said, "Do you know who the father is?"'

'Darling Alison. Tactful as ever.'

'She seemed to think it was a perfectly reasonable question. She said she did and that he would be delighted when he knew. That was one reason I was so sceptical of this alleged engagement but I couldn't say anything without breaking a confidence.'

'You didn't think she meant Ben?'

'He's eighteen and soon off to university. When you were going up to Oxford what would you have felt if a girl had told you she was pregnant by you?'

'Utter incredulity, since at eighteen I was an innocent virgin.'

'Don't be so literal. Use your imagination. You would hardly have described yourself as delighted, would you?'

'She may simply have been mistaken. If she thought he was that keen on her. I don't suppose she really grasped what it meant, his going away to university. Which doctor did she see?'

'That new one, Ned Savage—of all the unsuitable names for a doctor. Tall, dark, and sets the female patients pulsating.'

'Then we'll have a word with him this morning.' He kissed her lightly on the forehead. 'Thanks. Can I bring you up any breakfast? Boiled egg? Toast? Bacon-egg-sausage-kidneys-fried-bread?'

'Ugh. Stop it, you sadist. I'm going back to sleep. See you later.'

'Much later, I should think. Don't make any firm plans for the next couple of weeks—not ones that include me anyway.'

NICK TOLD BILL of the latest development when they met at the copse. 'People seem to confide in Alison, God knows why,' he said. 'It's not as if she's very sympathetic.'

'She's the lady of the manor now,' Bill said, surprisingly. 'Old habits die hard.'

'You *are* joking?'

'Not really. The villagers have been taking their problems to the big house for generations. Things don't

change overnight just because someone invented social workers.' Nick could think of no reply to this and
was silent. 'Miss Hope would know anyway—about
practical things, I mean,' Bill said obscurely. Nick de-
duced that he meant how to fix up a termination.

'Here's the spot where we found the body,' Bill said.
'You see how thick the copse is here. She could con-
ceivably have lain there for weeks, but for the dog.'

Nick looked around carefully. He had known the
place all his life but he tried to view it through fresh
eyes.

'Imagine trying to find any evidence here,' he sighed.
'Who was the SOCO?'

'Cruickshank, hindered by Harrison.'

'Well, that's something. If there's anything here,
George Cruickshank will have found it.

'What are the access points to this copse?' Nick
asked rhetorically. 'The hill paths up from The Hopfords and the lay-by on the moors. Who comes up here
at night? No one in their right mind. It's not even a
recognised rendezvous for lovers. It's got a bit of a
reputation, hasn't it? Not many people care to come up
here after dark.'

'You don't believe all them old witchcraft stories,
surely?'

'I didn't say that I, personally, was frightened to
come up after dark,' Nick said haughtily, 'but it was a
meeting place for covens right up until the end of the
eighteenth century.'

'Oh, as recently as that,' Bill said with considerable
sarcasm. Nick clutched his arm and let out a howl.

'What!' Bill yelped.

'It's Walpurgisnacht next week, Thursday. The great witches' sabbath. I'll leave you alone up here that night.'

'Stop playing silly buggers,' Bill said grumpily. 'It's not funny.'

'No.' Nick sobered up suddenly. 'It isn't. Let's go and see Dr Savage and I'll take a look at the body. Then I'll talk to Mrs Swift.'

You had to take your chances of humour where you found them. It shocked the public to see policemen chortling at the scene of a fatality—be it road accident, suicide or murder—as one of their number cracked a macabre joke. It shocked the cadets too. Until their tenth or fifteenth or twentieth corpse when they found themselves joining, however unwillingly, in the merriment. It was gallows humour—fingertip clinging to the cliff edge of what was normal and good and sane. Both men had seen too many corpses—women, children, their own colleagues even—to allow this one to depress them unduly but Nick who had known and liked Frisco, felt vaguely responsible while Bill's own exasperating and adored teenage daughters refused to be exorcised from his mind. Dr Edward Savage, who was a newcomer to the valley, might have stepped off the cover of a romantic novelette. He was twenty-eight, tall and handsome with a soulful look in his eyes and interesting bags under them. Perhaps being a doctor was even more stressful than being a copper, Nick speculated, or perhaps Savage was just young, idealistic and over-zealous. His name was inappropriate in every way—more aesthete than savage, he was Adonis after a sleepless night.

'Yes,' he said when they had explained the situation to him. 'She came to see me last Wednesday afternoon. I did a test and asked for it to be given priority. She doesn't even look after herself properly so I thought if she was pregnant and decided to keep the baby, I'd make her come to antenatal classes if I had to drag her by the hair.'

'So when did you get the results?'

'I'll check with my receptionist or would you rather speak to her yourself?' Nick, who didn't have an hour to spare listening to his Aunt Avis, let Savage go off on the errand. He was back in a few minutes.

'They came in on Saturday. It was positive.'

'So she'd had it confirmed by the time she died on Sunday night,' Nick said.

'Well . . . no. I don't allow the results of pregnancy tests to be given over the phone. Saturday is emergencies only, so I had told her to come back early this week.'

'You said if she decided to keep it. Did she bring up the subject of abortion?'

'No, she seemed quite happy about it all, in fact.'

'Did you ask who the father was?'

'No, and she made no reference to him at all. At least, I said would he stand by her? And she said that he would.'

'SO,' NICK SAID as Bill pulled the car up in front of the mortuary, 'she hadn't had it confirmed. So did she tell the man that night or not? If not, we're back looking for another motive.'

'It's got to have something to do with it surely,' said Bill, who wasn't about to give up such an obvious motive.

'Who knew she *might* be pregnant?' Nick asked. 'Frisco herself, Alison, Dr Savage and possibly the father. Who knew for sure? No one. Not even Savage, who had to go and check that the results were back. I think this pregnancy is a red herring. Damn and blast!' He got out of the car and took a few deep breaths. 'All right,' he said. 'Let's get it over with.'

A few minutes later Nick was staring down at the white, still face of Frisco Carstairs.

'What sort of maniac could do such a thing?' he asked despairingly.

'Happens all the time,' Bill said. 'Makes you wonder why you ever let your daughters out of your sight. You knew her, sir?'

'Yes, I knew her well. She used to do a bit of gardening for us.'

Frisco had been an erratic but gifted gardener. She couldn't be bothered with weeding or digging but half-dead plants rose like Lazarus under her grubby fingers. She had no sense of time and you never knew when she was going to turn up. Often Nick would wake up in the morning early and go out on to the balcony and see Frisco wandering round the grounds in the morning dew, barefoot as often as not. It saddened him to think that he would never see her there again. He realised that Bill was speaking.

'Sorry, Bill, what did you say?'

'I said it was a funny sort of name, Frisco. Is it short for something?'

'San Francisco, believe it or not.'

'Blimey!'

'She was born right in the middle of all the flower-power stuff, remember? "If you're going to San Francisco, be sure and wear a flower in your hair"?' Bill smiled suddenly and Nick, who had been a spotty schoolboy in 1967, realised that Bill had been in the prime of young manhood at that time. There were obviously some fond memories lurking but now was not the time to tease him about them. Bill caught his boss's eye and speedily rearranged his features.

'Rumour had it that her dad was an American soldier from one of the local bases,' Nick went on. 'Iris Carstairs ran off two years later with another soldier. Frisco was raised by her grandmother who died a couple of years ago.'

'Someone said the girl was simple.'

'I'm not so sure. She couldn't write and could barely read. The school said she was backward, of course, but Alison has always maintained that she wasn't, just stubborn and unbiddable—didn't want to learn, so she didn't. She was biddable enough where men were concerned though.'

'Oh yeah, there was a prosecution, wasn't there? When she was fourteen or fifteen.'

'The only surprising thing about that was that there was only one.'

'Shouldn't she have been in care, or something?'

'By the time her grandmother died, she was seventeen. I expect the social services had better things to do than fuss over a girl who would no longer be a minor in a few months.'

'What is she then, nineteen? Twenty?'

'Yes. That must be right. Nineteen.'

SIX

OLD MILL HOUSE might have come off a jigsaw box—
Olde England at its most winsome. It stood on the
banks of the Hop outside Great Hopford; its mill wheel
still moving slightly in the current; its shutters freshly
painted. A labrador puppy pounced confidently on
Nick's feet as he got out of the car. Apple blossom was
beginning to show in the orchard.

The Swifts employed a full-time housekeeper, a
black-widow Spanish woman, who showed Nick and
Bill wordlessly into the over-upholstered drawing room.

Penelope Swift rose to greet them, shook hands with
Nick and nodded graciously to Bill—a nice social distinction, Nick thought wryly. She was a well-preserved
forty, many years younger than her husband whose
second wife she was. She was dressed expensively but
without imagination. She might have been an athlete
once—her handshake was strong—but the muscles
were beginning to soften. And her breath smelt of
peppermints. Under the peppermint Nick detected
something of the warm sweet milky smell of puppy. He
warmed to her for the first time in their intermittent
acquaintance.

A more hesitant athlete now, he thought gently. It
was no wonder that she and Alison clashed—two such
indomitable women. But whereas Alison had har-
nessed her strength and mastered it and bent it to her
will, Penny Swift gave him a feeling of strength wasted

or misapplied—of a boxer about to knock himself out
for the count.

'Will you take tea?' she asked. It was the same
forceful voice that could be heard any day at Wimble-
don or Ascot, happy for anyone to know its business,
having nothing to hide. Except a few empty bottles. 'I
know it isn't a social call but we may be civilised,
mayn't we?'

'Thank you, Mrs Swift.'

'Tea for three, Mercedes,' she told the housekeeper.
'Do sit down, Mr Trevellyan. And how is dear Alison?'

'Very well indeed, thank you.'

'Such a help with the fête. So useful to have such a
willing little helper.' Nick merely smiled. Bill made an
odd noise in his throat which caused Penelope Swift to
look at him sharply. He coughed.

'Excuse me,' he said. 'Hay fever season starting.'

'Isn't that rather inconvenient in your job?'

'Yes, madam,' Bill agreed obligingly.

The Spanish woman brought in a tray and Nick rose
to take it from her. Penny Swift poured three cups of
very weak china tea and added a thin slice of lemon to
each. Bill examined his dubiously and left it on the
coffee table.

'I'm sorry to make you go over all this again, Mrs
Swift,' Nick began.

'I made a full statement at the time, of course.'

'Thank you. I often find that some details can spring
to mind a few days after an incident, or that the right
questions may bring them out. I realise it must be dis-
tressing for you.'

'Not really. I didn't know the girl.'

'Oh? But she'd lived in Little Hopford all her life.'

'Well, by sight perhaps but you know how it is. People who aren't . . . who don't move in the same social circles.'

'Yes. I see.'

'I don't want to seem callous but the girl was simpleminded.'

'You did know her then,' Nick said, 'to speak to.'

'What?'

'You knew she was simple?'

'Well, I don't know. All right, she used to hang about a bit. In the village, on the moors.'

'You go up there much?'

'Almost every day. The dog, you know. Labby.'

'Of course. She's just a puppy, isn't she?'

'Why, yes.'

'I expect you've had a lot of them over the years,' Nick said politely. 'Like Lady Armitage and her spaniels.'

'Oh yes, dear Molly. It's nice to have company on a country walk. The children are away at school, you see, and Giles is up in London so much.'

'Of course,' Nick said with sympathy. He was seeing Penelope Swift for the first time as a lonely woman, isolated by the scarcity of people eligible for her 'social circle', limited by a wall of her own building. Alison Hope the vicar's daughter and successful businesswoman must have seemed heaven sent—at first. No wonder she had grown to hate Alison so much.

'Do you always walk that way, Mrs Swift,' he asked.

'Not always, but it's a nice walk and the nearest to Great Hopford. It's about the right length for Labby as she's not fully grown.' She paused then said evenly, 'I don't quite see what you're getting at.'

'I merely wondered how well you knew the copse, Mrs Swift. Whether you'd notice anything different about it.'

'I see. I'm not really a very noticing person.'

'DRINKING LADY,' Bill said as they got back into the car twenty minutes later.

'Oh?' Nick said provocatively.

'Didn't you smell the peppermints?'

'So she likes peppermints. It's not a crime.'

'You aren't half naive sometimes,' Bill began. Then he caught Nick's eye and flushed. 'Oh, very funny,' he said.

'Don't be too hard on her, Bill. Life's not that easy for women of her age and class.'

'You what! All the pleasures of marriage and motherhood and none of the work. Housekeepers, boarding schools for the kids. My Susie—'

'Boredom,' Nick broke in. 'Mind numbing boredom and loneliness. The Colonel's away a lot and mostly from choice from what I can make out. Your Susie isn't lonely and she doesn't have time to be bored. She's too busy ironing your shirts and the girls' school uniforms and feeding you all...and loving you all.' Penny Swift didn't even have the Whitsun fête to organise any more.

'I suppose,' Bill conceded the point grudgingly. 'You feel sorry for the poor cow, don't you?'

'Mmm,' Nick said, non-committally. He felt sorry for the poor cow.

'I HATE this house-to-house stuff,' Detective Constable Paul Penruan grumbled. 'You've been in this game longer than me, Carol, have you ever known it turn anything up?'

DC Carol Halsgrove shrugged. 'The one time we skimped on it would be the one time it was vital,' she said philosophically.

'The Corpse in the Copse,' Penruan said. He liked the sound of the phrase and tried it again more slowly. 'The Corpse in the Copse. Do you think the papers would buy that as a headline?'

'Shut up,' Carol said. 'Or I shall make you walk back to Hopbridge.'

'My feet are killing me. And if I ever see another cup of stewed tea, I shall get homicidal myself.'

'Stop moaning. At least they haven't dragged you back from your leave like the guv'nor.'

'I wasn't moaning exactly. I'm just not sure it's the best use of resources.'

'I look forward to seeing changes when you're Chief Constable then, thickhead,' Carol said unkindly. 'I just radioed in and the sarge said we could call it a day.'

'Great.' Penruan wrenched open the driver's door of the car.

'I'll drive!' Carol said hurriedly. Paul submitted gracefully and got into the passenger seat. He pulled down the sun visor and admired himself in the vanity mirror on the back of it.

'I bet Nick's not best pleased at being called in,' he said. 'I wouldn't be if I was supposed to be on holiday with Alison Hope.'

'Since Alison has eyes only for him and has hardly noticed your existence, you're quite safe from that particular disappointment.'

'You know, I never thought Nick Trevellyan had it in him.'

'In that case,' Carol said scathingly, 'you must be even more stupid than I thought.'

Penruan looked hurt. 'It's just that he'd always struck me as a bit of a cold fish.'

'When he and Lucy Fielding were lovers, she didn't exactly look as if she was going to make a complaint under the Trades Descriptions Act.'

'She's gorgeous,' Penruan said with a sigh. 'When I was at the Comprehensive, Lucy Fielding was the sexual fantasy of half the sixth form. The other half was the girls—and I'm not sure some of them didn't have the hots for her too. Do you think she's too old for me?'

'A twelve-year-old would be too old for you,' Carol said.

They reached Hopbridge and Carol garaged the car behind the police station.

'Fancy a drink?' Paul asked suddenly.

'Why?'

He looked startled. 'I've got nothing better to do.'

'Maybe I have.'

'Do you want a drink or not?'

'Oh, all right. I'm not doing anything special.'

Carol didn't mind being in the pub with Penruan. It was good for her image to be seen with such a good-looking boy. She thought of him as a boy although he was only three or four years her junior. She didn't dislike him—he was too good-natured for that, just not very bright. He bought her a vodka and tonic and sat down on the bench next to her.

'Not got a date tonight?' she asked him. He shook his head. 'How come?' He shrugged. 'Can't find yourself a date?' she teased. 'Or have you been through all the glamorous blondes in the West Country?'

'I know you don't think much of me, Carol,' he said humbly, making her feel as if she'd just tripped up a cripple.

'Oh, come on!' she said. 'Can't you take a bit of teasing?' Carol had three older brothers and you wouldn't have survived in her family by being over-sensitive. Penruan just had a widowed mother and young sister who thought the sun shone out of his eyes.

'Sometimes I think Nick Trevellyan will get me transferred out of CID,' he said suddenly.

'Oh,' Carol said uncertainly. 'I don't think he'll do that.' She crossed her fingers under the table.

'He's always telling me I should watch you and be-have as you do. Would you help me? I couldn't bear to be chucked out of CID and back into uniform.'

'Well, I don't know what I can do,' Carol said. 'I'll help if I can but I can't give you a brain transplant.'

'Everyone's so clever,' he said, 'You, Nick, even Bill. For all he seems so slow and solid, he doesn't miss much.'

Carol squeezed his hand. 'I'll help if I can, Pen-ruan. On condition that you cut out the self-pity.'

'Thanks.' He squeezed her hand back. 'Want an-other drink or do you fancy a curry?'

'OK,' she said. 'But make it a Chinese.'

'Done.'

'THERE YOU ARE!' Dr Brewster said, barging into Nick's office half an hour later. 'I've been after you all day. Don't you have minions to do the leg work?'

'Bill and I are minions,' Nick explained. 'Ask Reg if you don't believe me. What are you so excited about, Mike?'

Mike waved a sheaf of papers at him. 'PM report. What do you think?'

'Let me guess. How about the corpse was pregnant.'

Dr Brewster, deflated, slumped down on a chair. 'You rotten sod,' he said.

'Sorry to spoil your fun. You can tell me how many weeks though.'

'Oh? Did the crystal ball not run to that? About seven.'

'Anything else of interest?'

'You could just read the report,' Mike said huffily.

'You could just tell me about it briefly then I might just buy you a pint.'

'Oh, well, in that case. She was an under-sized kid but surprisingly healthy...apart from being dead, that is,' Mike added, with what sounded suspiciously like a chortle. 'Er...sorry. Occupational hazard, callousness.'

'Ours too. Not like you to apologise for it though. You must be desperate for that pint.'

'Death by strangulation, not manual, almost certainly that scarf,' Mike recited. 'No other signs of violence. It must all have been very quick. I'd say she didn't put up much of a fight.'

'Get any semen?'

'Yes.' Mike's eyes lit up with enthusiasm. 'Lovely specimen. Your murderer was blood group O.'

'The man she was with that evening,' Nick corrected. 'We'll decide when we've got him in custody if he was the murderer or not.'

Mike shrugged. 'Why complicate matters? She's not the first girl to die that way and she won't be the last. Find your lover and you'll have your murderer.'

'Maybe. Blood group O, you say. Couldn't you have made it something less common?'

'It could have been A which is even more common in this part of the country. I'd say roughly a third of all the men in the valley are group O.'

'I'm group O myself,' Nick said. 'Same as the rest of the family.'

'Just be thankful you're not looking for your murderer among the Cherokee Indians,' Mike said cheerfully. 'They're all group O.'

Nick got up hastily. 'If you're going to deliver your lecture on blood groupings we'd better go straight to the Eagle where I won't be able to hear it so well.'

'Not implying I'm a bore on the subject, are you?' Mike asked, unoffended. 'Lead me to the watering trough.'

'Just a quick one, mind.'

'It always is these days. So how is the delicious Alison?'

'Very well, thank you.'

'You always come up smelling of roses, don't you? All the pleasures of marriage and none of the pitfalls, eh?'

'That's one way of looking at it.'

'Domestic bliss seems to suit you. You've even put on a bit of weight. You soon won't be able to hide behind lamp-posts any more.'

'I may soon have to let the belt out a notch,' Nick agreed.

'You see, the bloody woman can even cook. And you're the faithful type, aren't you?'

'You make me sound like a golden retriever. But if you mean that since I've got a beautiful, intelligent, funny, affectionate, passionate woman at home why should I go out looking for spare?—then, yes, I am the faithful type. And so are you.'

'That's a vile calumny.'

'Do you know what Helen said to me once? She said, "Mike likes to think he's an old rake and all the time he's a domestic boot-scraper."'

Mike laughed happily. 'The bitch! I'll black her eye for her when I get home.'

'Do you want that pint or not?'

Mike got up. 'Coming for a quick one, William?'

'No thanks, Doc. I'll go home and see if the kids remember who I am.'

'Wish I was single again,' Mike said with a sigh as he followed Nick out of the room.

'Not to mention twenty years younger,' Nick said unkindly.

PENRUAN WAS better company than Carol had expected. As they ate their dinner he told her some funny stories about his cadet training and she swopped them for horror stories about Superintendent Seymour at HQ.

'I'm surprised our super doesn't call HQ in more often,' Penruan said. 'After all, Nick Trevellyan is pretty junior to head murder enquiries.'

'Reg Grey's no fool,' Carol told him, 'despite appearances to the contrary. He knows that the guv'nor solves crimes whereas Seymour just arrests people.' She could see from Penruan's strained look that the subtlety of the distinction was too much for him.

'Seymour arrests the most obvious person,' she explained impatiently. 'Nine times out of ten they did it and everyone says how wonderful he is. The tenth time their brief tears him to shreds. Except it isn't him in the witness box on those occasions. It's always poor old Tony Cartwright.'

Inspector Tony Cartwright was neither particularly old—late thirties—nor especially poor. A large mournful-looking man, his life was divided between being Ted Seymour's scapegoat at work and his wife's whipping boy at home. Carol had ended up in bed with him one tipsy evening, during her years at Headquarters, mainly because she felt so sorry for him. It had been a disaster. She didn't feel like confiding any of this to Penruan so she just said: 'Nick arrests people only when he's worked it all out and he's sure.

'Besides,' she persisted, jabbing a forkful of noodles in Penruan's general direction, 'Nick would have made Chief Inspector before now if only he wasn't so bloody-minded. Every time I see him scrapping with Reg Grey, I think—there goes another promotion board where he won't make DCI. Sometimes I think he doesn't bloody care.'

'WHOEVER THE MAN WAS he was a secretor,' Nick told Alison that night.

'What?'

'Most men are. It means we can identify his blood group from his sperm. He's group O.'

'Pretty common, isn't it?'

'Yes, but at least it's some help. If I can get blood and sperm samples we can narrow it down to men with the right blood group who are also secretors. I'll tell you something else,' he added, 'something which occurred to me on Wednesday, only it slipped my mind afterwards what with going to Venice. Ben said he'd spent the afternoon in Hopbridge buying Frisco's engagement ring, but she couldn't have been with him because she was here that afternoon, remember, planting tomato seedlings. She didn't leave here until four and we now know that she went straight to see Dr Savage.'

'Ben didn't say she'd been with him.'

'No, we just assumed it. It is usual for a girl to go and choose her own engagement ring these days, isn't it? Don't you find it a bit odd that she let him choose it by himself?'

Alison shook her head. 'I told you, I'm sure she had no intention of marrying Ben, so it was immaterial to her what the ring was like. Didn't you see her wink at me in the pub? When Dot made that big scene it was as if that was what Frisco had been hoping for. She looked really pleased with herself. You can't tell me she would have looked like that if Dot was really going to be her mother-in-law.'

'Then what was the point of it all?'

'I think she just wanted to get at Dot. Dot's got a sharp tongue, you know, and Frisco's felt the edge of it more than once. She might think it was a good practical joke to let Dot think that she'd spoilt all her plans for her precious son. And it worked, didn't it?'

'Only too well perhaps. Her practical joke may have cost her her life. Wasn't it a bit hard on Ben?'

'Frisco doesn't think like that. If it crossed her mind at all, she would just think that Ben would soon find someone else and get over it. As, of course, he would have done. If she was using Threeoaks Copse to meet another man, like when you saw her there on Tuesday afternoon say, then she probably met the same man there on Sunday night.'

Nick considered this. 'Or she might have met Ben Lawson there on Sunday night and he might not have taken his dismissal as lightly as she expected.'

Alison spread her hands in a gesture of hopelessness. 'With a girl like Frisco something like this was almost bound to happen. Running around with men she hardly knew, in dark places—' She caught the look on Nick's face and tailed off.

'She had it coming to her?' he asked coolly. 'Is that what you mean, Ms Feminist-Businesswoman?'

'No! Well, I mean—' It was not often that Alison found herself at a loss for words.

'She was just a naive, trusting kid,' Nick said angrily. 'I liked her.'

'So did I—'

'You didn't have to look at her poor swollen face, her blue lips, the marks on her neck, the soil under her finger nails where she scrabbled in the dirt before she died!' He shuddered at the memory of that bloated face whose likeness now stared at him from every wall of the incident room.

Alison was ashamed and could still think of no reply. Nick took her silence for anger. He got up and walked out of the house, shutting the front door loudly behind him.

'Sod you and your woolly-liberal conscience,' Alison muttered, as she heard the Ford splutter into life. Nick spent the night at his flat which he often—sometimes—did when he was working on a case, as it was so handy for his office.

SEVEN

ALTHOUGH NICK HAD BEEN a witness to the scene in the Bird in Hand on Wednesday night, he had no means of knowing what had happened after the mass exit of the Lawsons. He was unconvinced that Ben and Frisco's engagement had anything to do with her murder, but he had nothing else to go on at that moment. So the following morning he and Bill set out to interview the other people who had been present that evening.

The first stop was at Dot and Sam Lawson's cottage in Church Path, Little Hopford. Sam opened the door. It must have been an unusual experience for him to open the door to a copper and not be arrested himself, Nick thought. He was in his shirt sleeves, the inevitable cigarette hanging out of his mouth. When he opened his mouth to speak the cigarette, to Nick's fascination, remained stuck to his lip.

'Got any identification?' he asked.

Dot appeared at the door behind him. 'Don't be so stupid, Sam. Come in, Mr Trevellyan.'

Nick asked them both to go down to the police station in Hopbridge but they refused.

'If you want to talk to us you can do it here,' Dot said. 'I told him,' she pointed at Bill for whom the instinctive dislike was obviously mutual, 'everything on Monday. I haven't got all day to be going into Hopbridge, Mr Trevellyan. It's my afternoon for cleaning for the Vicar in Great Hopford. If you want to take us down to the station you'll have to arrest us. I know my rights.' Nick gave in gracefully and accepted Dot's offer of a cup of tea as a sign of truce.

'Alison went away a bit sudden this time, didn't she?' Dot said as she poured it.

'Yes,' Nick said abruptly. He had gone to Hope Cottage first thing that morning to ask Alison's forgiveness for transferring his irrational guilt on to her but there had been no sign of her and Dot had just confirmed his worst fears.

'Only she never said when I saw her yesterday morning—just dropped me a note through my door last night.'

'Something came up. She had to nip to town.' It was a common enough occurrence. Alison frequently went Bunburying in London although she called it Networking. As far as Nick could make out it consisted of having long, boozy lunches with other businesswomen. Dot didn't see anything odd in it.

'And you prefer to sleep at your flat when she's not there, I know. Place too big and empty for you.'

'That's right.'

'Only she wants me to springclean the kitchen and bathroom while she's away.'

'Mmmm,' Nick grunted unhelpfully.

'How long's she gone for?'

Nick sipped his tea and considered. 'Not more than a couple of days, I shouldn't think. Let's get on, shall we?'

Bill was drinking his tea with rather more relish than he had brought to Mrs Swift's pale brew although the look on Dot's face suggested that she might have slipped something nasty into it. He put his cup down reluctantly and took out his notebook.

Nick had told Bill to ask the questions, while he watched the reactions of the witnesses. So he chose a seat in an unobtrusive corner while Bill sat down at the table. Although Bill did the talking, Dot addressed her answers to Nick all the way through the interview as if she imagined that he was the ventriloquist and Bill Deacon his dummy.

'You know that the body of Miss San Francisco Carstairs,' Bill studied his notebook as though double checking this unlikely name, 'was found in Threeoaks Copse on Monday morning and that she is believed to have been murdered there some time on Sunday night.'

'Course we do,' Lawson said. 'It was you that came here that morning and told us, and I told you then and I'm telling you now, you're not pinning this one on my boy.'

'No one's trying to pin anything on anyone,' Bill said reasonably. 'We just want to get at the truth. When I spoke to you before you didn't tell me about the incident in the pub last Wednesday night.'

'Didn't seem much point,' Dot said, 'since you were there yourself at the very time, Mr Trevellyan.'

'Mr Trevellyan was present at the scene in the saloon bar, Mrs Lawson. I want you to tell me what happened after you, your husband and your two sons left the bar.'

'I'll tell you what happened—I boxed his ears good and proper like you saw, Mr Trevellyan, that's what happened and then I brought him home and he's not been let out since. I was gonna send him away to my sister in Bristol for a few days and that was to be an end to the nonsense. Well, it's certainly ended now and I'm not going to pretend I'm sorry. It was bound to happen sooner or later. Little slut!'

'She wasn't a slut,' said a voice from the doorway. Ben had arrived during his mother's tirade, unnoticed by anyone except Nick. 'You shouldn't talk about her that way.' His voice caught and for a moment Nick thought he was going to burst into tears. Dot looked at her youngest son, her baby, with a more tender expression than Nick had ever seen on her face. The boy, for he looked no more than a child, was tormented, his dark curls uncombed, his huge brown eyes circled with sleeplessness.

'Well, love,' she said, 'at least you can be grateful I didn't let you out again. Mr Trevellyan will know you couldn't have had anything to do with it.'

Nick sensed a tensing of the atmosphere. It was coming from Sam's direction. He didn't know quite what it was—Sam's sweat glands stepping up production probably.

He said gently, 'But you did see her again, didn't you, Ben? On Sunday night, was it?'

Ben nodded dumbly. Dot was on her feet in an instant and turning on Sam. 'I told you not to let him go out. The minute my back's turned—'

Bill Deacon tried desperately to regain control of the situation. 'In your statement on Monday, Mrs Lawson, you said you were here all Sunday evening with your husband and son. Do you now wish to change that statement?'

'I had to go out to clear up after Mrs Dixon's drinks party on Sunday. Sam was here.'

'So it wasn't true that your son was with you all evening?'

'Sam was here, I tell you. It's the same thing or should have been. I told him not to let him out, Mr Trevellyan.'

'The boy's young, Dot,' Sam mumbled. 'I couldn't see any harm in him having a bit of fun.'

'I'll give you bit of fun—'

For a moment it looked as if a fist fight was about to break out between husband and wife. Nick got up from his chair and banged on the table making them both jump.

'That's enough!' he said angrily. 'Sit down and shut up, Dot. And I'll have the truth from now on.'

The look Dot gave Nick accorded ill with Alison's assertion that she had a soft spot for him. Nick ignored her and went over to Ben. 'So you saw her on Sunday, Ben. What time was it? It's very important for us to establish what time she died, you see.'

Ben wiped his shirt sleeve across his moist eyes. 'Mum went out at half past eight. Frisco must have been watching for her to go. She came to the door. I knew Dad wouldn't make any trouble for me with Mum. We just went for a walk. I left her at about nine-thirty to be sure to get back here before Mum.'

'A walk, you say? Where did you go?'

'Just as far as her cottage. I'd brought her a present I wanted to give her—a scarf. I brought it Wednesday when I got the ring but I forgot to give it to her then.'

'Did you have sexual relations with her that night, Ben?' Nick asked seriously. 'Think carefully before you answer. You must tell me the truth.'

'No.' There was no hesitation. 'She wasn't like that, Mr Trevellyan, honest she wasn't. She said we must wait until we were married.'

Dot snorted. Nick stared at him incredulously.

'If you're going to tell lies, Ben, you might at least make them plausible.'

'I'm not lying! I'm not! I'm not!'

Nick was momentarily at a loss. Every instinct told him that the boy was telling the truth.

'All right, Ben,' he said. 'What was it like, this scarf?'

'Sort of mauve colour with yellow flowers. She said she liked it. She put it on straight away, round her neck, and gave me a kiss to thank me.'

Sam Lawson confirmed that he had seen Frisco at eight-thirty when she had called for Ben but not at nine-thirty when he had been engrossed in his favourite television programme.

'All right,' Nick said. 'That will do for now.' He got as far as the door and then turned back to Ben. 'So,' he said deliberately, 'you maintain that the child she was carrying couldn't be yours?'

Ben gaped at him for a second, then burst into tears at last.

'It's not true. I don't believe you. It isn't true.'

'I want you down the station again, Ben. I want a blood sample and a sperm sample.' Nick took the boy's arm gently. Dot leapt up.

'It's not right. He's just a child.'

'No, he isn't. You're over seventeen, aren't you Ben?'

'Eighteen last February,' Ben said miserably.

'That makes him an adult, by any criterion.' Dot gave Nick a poisonous look and said she wanted a solicitor. Somehow Nick didn't think Hope Cottage was going to get its springclean.

ALISON HAD ARRANGED to meet her old friend, Ralph Squires, for lunch that day at a fashionably over-priced restaurant in Covent Garden. They had been at Cambridge together and Alison, who had had a crush on Ralph in her first year, had kept up with him for old times' sake.

Ralph was late as always and Alison settled comfortably at the bar to await his entrance. Ralph had been the University Theatre Club's leading man for two years and his arrival in any place had to be carefully timed. Alison watched dispassionately as he finally came in. He had been a very handsome boy, tall and athletic with blond good looks. She'd always had a weakness for big blonds—oddly enough, since Nick was thin and dark. Now the signs of soft living and over-indulgence were only too clear in Ralph. The dry skin was laced with fine lines and the big blue eyes were bloodshot. He was looking around him with a world-weary air so Alison gave him a little wave to attract his attention.

'Alison darling.' He kissed her on the cheek, signalling for the barman as he did so. 'How *healthy* you look. Must be all that country air. Such rosy cheeks.' Privately he thought that she looked windblown and coarse. He settled on a bar stool next to her, gulped down a large gin and tonic and signalled for another. Only when that was safely in his hand did he turn his attention back to Alison and bestow his sexiest smile on her. He had known that Alison Hope (Scholarship girl, Girton) had had a crush on him and liked to assume, in the teeth of all the evidence to the contrary, that she still had one twelve years later. He leant towards her. His breath was not quite fresh and she had to stop herself from drawing back. It occurred to her how thankful she was that he had taken no notice of her that first year at Girton, heart-breaking as it had been at the time.

'When are you going to give up this country nonsense and come back to civilisation?' he was saying.
'Or if you had to live in the country why not somewhere decent, like the Cotswolds? A joke's a joke but
I thought for sure you'd have tired of it by now. What
do you do for fun down there?'

'It wasn't a joke. I like the country, I like my new
life. I'm working better than ever before—taking on
new people, expanding in all directions.'

'And I suppose whatsizname is still in evidence—the
country bobby.'

'Nick's just fine. I'll tell him you asked after him.
He'll be thrilled. How's Charlotte?'

On leaving Cambridge Ralph had married rather
well—'Money and breeding, darling,' he had told Alison at the time. The Honourable Charlotte Turnbull
was the daughter of a political life peer whose family
were in merchant banking. Ralph had been welcomed
into the family as a beautiful and bright young man
and offered a job in the bank. He had not adapted well
to City life and had soon fallen out with his in-laws. He
had agreed to leave the firm quietly if some of Dad-
dy's money could be found to start him up in the an-
tique business. He and Charlotte lived in high style,
entertaining often and lavishly and spending a good
deal of money.

'It's a sore point,' Ralph was explaining. 'She's
gone, left me. Or rather kicked me out. She's got the
kids and the house.' Since Charlotte's father had
bought them the house as a wedding present this did
not strike Alison as unreasonable. She showed a suitable amount of concern but Ralph required no encouragement to pour out his grievances.

'There've always been other women—she knew that. Why did she want to go and kick up a fuss this time? It's so middle-class to bother about things like that. Of course her father's only a life peer—it's not real breeding, is it? I'm living in some dump of a flat just round the corner from here—off Drury Lane.'

The waiter was hovering, anxious for them to take their table, so Alison steered Ralph away to the dining room. She had no intention of letting him spoil the whole meal, wallowing in self pity. She decided to tell him about Frisco to take his mind off his own troubles. He was interested.

'You should have told me about her when I came down to stay. She sounds like a good sort.'

'By which you mean an easy lay. You did meet her, she's the girl who does our garden—did our garden, I should say.'

'Oh, I see. Her.' Ralph lost interest.

'She was a bit inclined to chase after men.'

'Including Nick?'

'I don't think so. He's quite capable of fending off unwanted attentions, if so. No, I think she looked on him as a sort of big brother—he was always very kind to her.' But then, he was kind to almost everyone.

'I bet!' Ralph said. 'You didn't use to be so naive, Alison.'

'Not every man is like you, Ralph. He says she doesn't look after herself properly so if he's there when she comes, he always makes her some breakfast and stands over her while she eats it.'

'Proper little social worker, isn't he?'

Alison giggled suddenly. 'Jake and Simon came to stay just before Christmas. Frisco propositioned both of them.'

'What, together?'

'No, separately. She took quite a fancy to Jake.'

'I bet that went down well.'

'I thought Simon was going to have a fit.'

'What happened?'

'I took her on one side and explained to her. She was very innocent in some ways. Not that she believed me— she just stared at me as if she thought I was off my head and said, "What, two men?" She still kept following Jake around like a puppy, anyway. Oh dear, I keep forgetting the poor kid's dead.' Alison picked up the wine bottle. A waiter instantly snatched it from her hand and topped up her glass. Alison nodded at him coolly and told Ralph about the scene in the pub.

'Is that the pub Mr Plod's uncle runs?' he asked.

'No, Nick's uncle runs that pub out on the cliffs, overlooking the bay. I'm talking about the Bird in Hand in the village, near my house. We went there one evening, remember?'

'Of course, I must have got mixed up. How useful to have an uncle who runs a pub. Has he got another one who's a bookie and one who's, let me see, a pawnbroker?'

'You really are a filthy snob, Ralph.'

She began to tell him about her new game, but they quickly got sidetracked onto his business. For the rest of the meal they talked income tax and VAT. Ralph was interested in work only insofar as it brought in money to maintain his lifestyle. Almost all his talk was of money and how much Charlotte was taking off him. Alison, who liked being rich but was not miserly, soon began to weary of it.

'If you have two loaves, sell one and buy a lily,' she murmured.

'What was that? I didn't quite catch it.'

She repeated it more loudly. 'It's an oriental saying. Nick told it to me.'

Ralph looked concerned. 'You see, I was right. This living in the sticks is affecting your mind.'

Alison just smiled.

It was past three when they finally left the restaurant. They stood awkwardly on the pavement for a moment as a sea of early tourists swirled round them and a group of young breakdancers raised the roof in the nearby piazza.

'My flat's only two minutes walk from here,' Ralph said, raising his voice to be heard. 'We could go back for some more coffee, talk about old times.' Alison laughed and shook her head. 'Mr Plod won't know,' he persisted.

'There won't be anything for him to know. I want to pop round and have a word with Jake while I'm in the area so I'll say goodbye.'

'Are you staying long in town?'

'Not long at all.' Tomorrow she would head back to civilisation. Back to Nick, who did not take infidelity as a matter of course.

'I was glad you rang up this morning actually,' Ralph said. 'I was going to call you to ask if I could pop down again one weekend.'

'Oh?' Alison said in surprise. Ralph had pronounced the Hop Valley to be 'Simply too quaint and old-fashioned' the previous autumn.

'Well,' he smiled sheepishly, 'I'm at a bit of a loose end since Charlotte gave me the elbow. I thought a few days' holiday might do me good—you know, cheer me up a bit.'

'Yes, of course,' Alison said sympathetically. 'Of course you can come, Ralph. Anytime.'

'It's been nice talking to you about my troubles. Thanks for being such a good listener. We go back a long way, you and me.'

'Mmm,' Alison said. 'I hope you and Charlotte can patch things up, Ralph.' She glanced at her watch. 'Well, give me a ring when you're coming. See you soon.'

'Thanks for the lunch.'

Alison slung her bag over her shoulder and headed off towards Long Acre. A young woman with a clipboard stepped out of a doorway in front of her.

'Excuse me,' she said, pen poised.

'Certainly,' Alison said, not breaking step.

The girl, with unexpected tenacity, trotted after her.

'Do you work at all?' she asked.

'Yes. I mind my own business.' Alison turned into the offices of Trowerbridge and Colman, her solicitors, and shut the door behind her.

EIGHT

ALAN LAWSON LIVED on an estate of just twelve detached houses, about half a mile out of Hopbridge to the east. The small front garden was neat and tidy, all lawn and shrubs for easy maintenance. A newish car stood well polished on the hard-standing in front of the double garage. At half past six that evening it was too light for the curtains to be drawn but nets obscured each window—even on the first floor. Bill pulled the car to a halt outside the house and examined it at his leisure.

'Bit posh for a schoolteacher, isn't it?' he said finally. 'They're always going on about how badly paid they are.'

'He's the deputy head,' said Nick who had been doing his homework. 'Head of Pastoral Care in the Upper School. I think that means he sorts out their personal problems. But I suspect you're right and that he lives at the limits of his income. Mind you, I should think his wife had a little bit saved, if she's anything like her father. Did you ever try getting an overdraft out of Terry Wilmott?'

Bill swung the car into the drive and Nick got out and walked up to the front door. Bill followed, muttering something about kids not having had personal problems in his day. They were expected and Mrs Lawson opened the door without waiting for their ring. She put a finger to her lips.

'Shh. I've just got the baby off.'

Nick's experienced eye took her in at a glance. He had met plenty of Angela Lawsons. Genus: respectable lower-middle (net curtain) class. Species: wife and mother; her features hardened by years of unpaid caring; her hair short to need, like the garden, the minimum of care. She was wearing dungarees—her third pregnancy now well advanced. She was not of the class to be nervous of the police. Nick, who knew her father—the bank manager—quite well, thought he could detect a touch of the Wilmott steel in the eyes and in the jut of her chin.

They tiptoed into the hall and followed her into a tiny book-lined room to the right of the front door, which she dignified by the name of "My Husband's Study".

"He's just finishing his supper. If you'd like to wait a moment he'll see you in here.' Her brisk tone implied that they could expect the same courtesies as travelling salesmen who had called about the double glazing.

Nick, who was accustomed both to being snubbed and to being kept waiting, made himself at home at the desk and began to leaf through a biology textbook. Bill went to examine some photographs of Hopbridge cricket club on the far wall.

'I bet you didn't know that you have the same number of bones in your neck as a giraffe,' Nick remarked.

'We did well last season,' Bill replied. 'Second in the league.'

'Do you think it'd be easy to break a giraffe's neck?'

'Penruan made fifty not out in the home match against Porlock.'

'You see. He does serve some purpose. You ask the questions, Bill. Okay?'

'Right you are.'

Alan Lawson joined them five minutes later. He knew both policemen by sight and offered them a limp and nervous hand. He was not a man who need fear the police, in theory—but there had been too many knocks on the door of his childhood in the terraced house in Church Path; too many occasions when self-assured men like these had come, once again, to take his father away.

Bill apologised politely for troubling him and began to question him while Nick took the opportunity to observe the younger man closely.

Alan Lawson was thirty but looked older. He already had the tiniest of bald patches, having that fair, wispy hair which recedes early. He spoke slowly and carefully, measuring each word—a man who has learned to slough off his native dialect in favour of BBC standards but is always in danger of slipping back. His manner was pompous; Nick mentally marked him down as the "What can I do for you, officers?" type.

'Well,' Alan said graciously, 'how can I help you, officers?' Not a bullseye, Nick thought, but definitely inner ring.

'We're investigating the death of Miss Carstairs on Sunday night, sir,' Bill began.

'So I understood from Inspector Trevellyan's telephone call earlier today, but I don't see how I can help you.'

'It appears that Miss Carstairs was engaged to be married to your youngest brother, Mr Benjamin Lawson,' Bill said. It was odd, Nick thought idly, how catching the pompous manner could be.

'Oh that,' Alan said, with a nervous laugh. 'Nobody took that seriously. They were just children.'

'Yet Mrs Lawson—your mother—thought their association sufficiently important to warrant a family conference. She did call you out to Little Hopford on Wednesday night, didn't she?'

'Well, yes, but it wasn't any sort of conference. Dad had just got home and she thought a family reunion was called for.'

'So she said nothing to you about your brother and Miss Carstairs, sir?'

Alan fingered his chin as he gave the question considerable thought. 'She did just mention it,' he said finally. 'That she had hardly seen Ben for a few days. That she was a bit worried. Vague stuff like that.'

Nick wasn't having that. 'Mr Lawson, are you telling me that you went out to Little Hopford just to buy your old dad a drink? He's a bit of an embarrassment to you, isn't he? I don't imagine your wife is very keen on your seeing him. You hardly ever come out to Little Hopford these days, do you?'

Patches of pink appeared on Alan Lawson's naturally pale complexion. 'I can't be blamed for my father's... peccadilloes. I don't know why I always have to have that thrown in my face.'

'I'm not throwing it in your face. I'm merely stating that you don't go to see your mother as a rule.'

'I don't get over as often as I'd like, no. Mother comes over here sometimes to see the kiddies.'

'Yet you maintain that Dot didn't ask you over to talk about Ben.'

'It was no big deal, I tell you, just one of those childish infatuations. He was due to go off to college soon. I thought it was a lot of fuss about nothing.'

'So you agree that Dot was making a fuss about it?'

Alan was at a loss and looked at Nick with a dislike which he could not conceal. Nick didn't pursue the matter, considering the point won. He nodded to Bill, who resumed his questioning.

'During the course of the evening your brother came into the Bird in Hand with Miss Carstairs. Can you tell us what happened next?'

'He came out with this nonsense about being engaged to Frisco—Miss Carstairs. Mum was furious, clouted him, dragged him off home. That's it really. You saw it all yourself.' He looked coldly at Nick.

'What did you think when your brother announced that he wanted to marry Miss Carstairs?' Bill asked.

'I thought he was a silly little fool, that Mum would put a stop to it, and that he'd soon get over it.'

'It seems someone broke the engagement off in the most decisive way possible.'

'Not anyone in my family I can assure you, Sergeant.' Alan rose to his feet. 'Now if you will forgive me I don't think I can be of any more help and I have a meeting this evening about timetable revisions for next term.'

Bill glanced at Nick then got up. Nick remained seated for a moment, looking at Alan Lawson, then he too rose. As Alan showed him to the door, Nick asked politely, 'Did you know Miss Carstairs yourself, sir?'

'Yes. She was at Hopbridge Comprehensive until about three years ago.'

'You knew her reputation?'

'Who didn't? She must have been killed by some man she picked up.'

He edged them adroitly to the front door and stood on the doorstep as they regained their car. 'I'm sure you'll find the guilty party, officers, please let me know if there's anything else I can help with.'

'Pompous git,' Nick said amiably, when he and Bill were safely back in the car.

'That wasn't much help,' Bill said. He gave Nick a look which said: He might have been more help if you'd let me do the talking and hadn't wound him up like that.

'He gets on my nerves,' Nick explained, reading the look easily. 'I don't like the way he's ashamed of his mother. Sorry.' Bill smiled and shook his head. 'Get off home, Bill. I don't think we can do much more tonight.' Bill didn't look particularly thrilled at the prospect. 'What's up? You're usually glad to get off.'

'Normally. But just tonight Susie's got tickets to see the Hopbridge Players in *Twelfth Night*. Sarah's doing it for GCSE next year.'

'I see what you mean. The Hopbridge Players are rather a fate worse than death, aren't they?'

'I dunno. I've never seen them. But I don't go much on Shakespeare. What's it about, this play?'

'It's about a woman everyone thinks is a man,' Nick said obscurely. 'She falls in love with a man who thinks she's a man and a woman falls in love with her, thinking she's a man.'

'Christ!' Bill said, wondering what sort of transvestite orgy he was letting himself in for.

'I'm not explaining it very well. I'm sure Sarah can do better. Alan Lawson would make a wonderful Malvolio, though.'

'Which of them is he?'

'None of them, another character altogether. Watch out for him.'

NICK RANG Hope Cottage, got the answering machine and slammed down the receiver in disgust. So he didn't bother to give himself the evening off but went back to the station and spent three hours catching up on paperwork and updating his report on the Carstairs murder. The inquest was fixed for the next morning and would be immediately adjourned.

His floor of the station was quiet and he was surprised when his door opened and Superintendent Grey put his head round. Nick got up.

'Sit, sit,' Reg said, also taking Nick for a golden retriever. 'I wanted a word, Nick.' He came in and sprawled on a chair. He was carrying a buff folder and various papers under his arm. He sat for a moment, apparently lost in thought.

Nick waited patiently. Reg Grey's moods had become a little unpredictable over the last couple of years. The fact that he had addressed Nick by his Christian name was a good sign.

'You're working late, sir,' he ventured just before the silence became oppressive.

'I've just come from a Rotarian meeting. I saw your light on and thought I'd look in as I was passing. Don't mind if I smoke in your office, do you?' Reg took one of his pipes from his pocket. Nick considered saying, truthfully, that he minded very much, but the moment passed and Reg had lit up.

'Good course? Good holiday?' he said, between puffs.

'I had a very good holiday.' Nick smiled, involuntarily, at the memory of Venetian siestas. 'The course was a bit bewildering. At this rate it won't be long before we just hand cases over to the forensic lab and the computers to solve while we become glorified filing clerks.'

'I don't know why you're always such a luddite.' Puff. Puff. 'Anyone would think you liked these sordid little murder cases.' Puff. 'That's what I wanted to talk about really—the Carstairs murder. I've read your preliminary report. Not much in it.'

'I don't know much,' Nick explained.

Reg fished out the report and scanned it quickly. He scratched his nose with the stem of his pipe. 'Just a few years ago people used to end reports to Superintendents with "I have the honour to be, sir, your obedient servant",' he told Nick, not for the first time.

'Yes, sir.' A few years ago, Nick thought, when Joan Collins was a teenager.

'I may have mentioned it before.'

'Once or twice perhaps.' Not for at least a fortnight though.

'Any thoughts?' Reg asked recovering from the nostalgia bout.

'Nothing really. It's not one of those obvious cases where we can make an arrest almost at once. I'm just going through the motions, quite frankly, and hoping that something will turn up.'

'Not the Lawson boy, then?'

'I don't think so. But I'm keeping an open mind for the time being. At least until I get the results of his tests back from the lab which won't be until tomorrow at the earliest. Forensic may turn something up from her clothes but it'll be at their own pace, of course.'

The Superintendent sat looking at him in silence for a moment. It was a habit which had given him the reputation of a contemplative man. Nick's own view was that he was just slow on the up-take. Reg spoke again at last.

'It sounds a pretty routine sort of case. Girl like that, easy lay.' Nick clenched his teeth to cage in the sharp retort which would otherwise have broken out and blasted Reg's pipe down his throat. 'No point in calling in any outside help at this stage, is there?' Reg went on, oblivious of his narrow escape.

'No, sir,' Nick said firmly.

'Did Dr Brewster manage to pin the time of death down?'

Nick made a face. 'Up to a point. It's cold at night at this time of year and there wasn't much warmth left in the body when he looked at it. But she'd had a meal of baked beans and bread not long before so Mike inclines to late Sunday evening. She was seen alive at nine-thirty so we're taking between ten and midnight as a working hypothesis.'

'And she was pregnant.'

'Yes. We already knew that but Mike was able to confirm it and say she was about seven weeks.'

'You mention her pregnancy in your preliminary report. How did you get on to that so fast?'

'Alison knew about it and Dr Savage confirmed it.'

'Oh,' Reg said coldly. 'Well, that brings me to the other thing.' He took the buff folder from under his arm and Nick recognised it as his own file.

'This file gives your address...' Reg opened it and read aloud '...as Flat 3, The White House, Market Square, Hopbridge.'

'Sir?'

'But it seems to be common knowledge that you're living out at Little Hopford. You know the regulations, Nick. Policemen may only live in places authorised by the Chief Constable and within easy reach of the station.'

'I'm not living there. At least ... not all the time. That's still my official address, the one in the file ... and Hope Cottage is only three miles from the station.' Nick was aware that some of these burblings were mutually exclusive but fairly confident that Reg wouldn't notice.

'We need to be able to get hold of you in an emergency, Nick.'

'Bill knows how to reach me. So does the desk.'

'I mean either you're living with that girl or not,' Reg persisted. He had suspected Alison of having murdered her cousin a few months earlier and he had never quite forgiven her for being so bloody-mindedly innocent. Besides, a young girl had no business being so assertive.

'Woman,' Nick said.

'Eh?'

'She's not a girl, she's a woman. She's thirty.'

Reg looked blank. 'Well, they none of them like getting older, do they? The little ladies.'

Nick decided against pursuing the point. 'It's not as simple as that,' he said instead.

Reg looked irritated. 'It was in my day,' he said flatly. 'When I found out about you and her, you gave me your word that she hadn't been your mistress while she was still under suspicion of murder.'

'That was the truth.' Nick covered his mouth to hide the smile brought on by Reg's outdated terminology. Although, come to think of it—

'I accepted your word then,' Reg was continuing, 'because not to do so would have laid you open to a very serious disciplinary charge. I gave you the benefit of the doubt.'

'I thought you accepted it because you believed me.'

'I didn't even say anything when you moved into her house a short time later,' Reg said, ignoring the interruption. 'I'm not doubting your word, Nick, but you're one of my best officers and I don't like to see you making a fool of yourself over a woman again.'

Nick raised his eyebrows. 'My God! Anyone would think I was Casanova.'

'I thought you'd learnt your lesson over that Fielding girl. I had to warn you then against associating with undesirables.'

'I don't want to go over that ground again, sir, it's ancient history.'

'You know there's been a big drug bust in Cornwall—a whole ring wound up?'

For a moment Nick thought, thankfully, that Reg was changing the subject. 'Yes, I heard.'

'Accounts for most of the cocaine flowing into the south west.'

'Good. They must be feeling very pleased with themselves.'

'One of the pushers picked up along the way was that tinpot, barrack-room-lawyer Bannister.'

'He's not a barrack-room-lawyer, he's a qualified solicitor—unfortunately.'

'You don't seem very surprised.'

'We've known for years he was an addict. It was only a matter of time before he started pushing.'

'He's a friend of the Fielding girl.'

'Not really a friend. In fact she doesn't like him.'

'Let's not split hairs. They belong to a lot of the same organisations. Subversive organisations.'

'I'm not sure what you're getting at,' Nick said. 'Lucy neither takes nor pushes drugs.'

'She's got too many friends from the wrong side of the tracks, Nick.'

'Look, Reg, I no longer have any connection with Lucy Fielding. I haven't even seen her for months. And surely you aren't suggesting that Alison qualifies as an undesirable person, are you? She's on first-name terms with the Chief Constable.'

'Don't get pert with me. Police officers need a stable home life. God knows they get enough excitement at work. This isn't London, the valley's an old-fashioned sort of place. Round here if people want to live together, they get married. Well, make sure you keep Records informed.' Reg rose to his feet to leave the office. He paused at the door.

'You can't have it both ways, Nick. If you aren't living at Hope Cottage then its distance from the station is irrelevant.' He swept out, jubilant in scoring a rare point off Nick.

Damn! Nick thought. He did notice. That was the trouble with Reg, he wasn't quite as stupid as he liked to make out.

'You needn't worry, Reg,' he said to the empty air, 'she isn't actually speaking to me at the moment.'

He got up and opened the window.

NINE

THE INQUEST WAS OPENED the next morning, with formal evidence of identification and cause of death being given, then adjourned for the police to pursue their enquiries. Nick was by no means sure in what direction to run in his pursuit, but he decided that the rest of the morning might best be spent on a visit to Frisco's cottage. Cruickshank and his team had given it the once over and he didn't expect to find any evidence there, but he felt that if he saw Frisco's habitat he might be able to fix her more clearly in his mind. So he changed out of his giving-evidence-in-court suit—the one which prompted some of his colleagues to ask if the pox doctor was in—and Bill drove him out to Little Hopford.

Nick had thought he knew Frisco. He had noticed her once or twice on his return to the valley three years ago: a teenage girl, old beyond her years physically and young below her years mentally, but oddly attractive, like a baby animal, a foal or a kitten. Since Alison, with her unerring nose for an expert, had bagged Frisco to help in the garden at Hope Cottage, he had come to know her well; to be concerned for her welfare; to find her undemanding company curiously relaxing.

As Bill unlocked the door he said, 'Who do you suppose her next of kin is, sir?'

'It must be her mother, assuming that she's still alive. No one's heard of her for years. I suppose we ought to do something about finding her, but the chances are that she's married, or changed her name at least. It's hard to know where to start.'

'I expect she'll see it in the papers and come forward.'

'It's an interesting point though, Bill. Frisco was worth something.' Bill looked surprised. 'Not much but something. She owns, owned, this cottage and the two others in the terrace.'

'How come?'

'Her grandmother owned them. It was a bit of a shock to everyone when she died and that came to light—people had naturally assumed that she just rented the place.'

'I remember her. The village wise woman, wasn't she?'

'Something like that. She made a proper will leaving it all to Frisco, though, so she didn't place all her reliance on herbs and magic spells.' It was safe to assume that Frisco had not taken similar precautions.

'Doesn't look worth much.' Bill looked round in dismay.

The cottage was a dirty, empty place. Nick was not surprised. Frisco had been a girl who travelled light through life. There were two rooms downstairs. The one at the front had faded curtains drawn across the windows and contained dusty furniture of pre-war vintage—old Mrs Carstairs' wedding purchases had seen out her and her entire lineage.

The back room seemed to be the one Frisco had used. There were ashes in the grate and a mattress on the floor. A pile of none too clean clothes lay higgledy-piggledy on a wooden chest. There was no make up, no scent, no costume jewellery—none of the usual icons of the young girl. No books, of course, but also no ornaments; no clocks or pictures, no family photographs.

A lean-to kitchen led off the room. A pint of sour milk stood on the table. The SOCOs might at least have got rid of that. Nick poured it down the sink and ran the single cold tap to disperse the solid curd.

'Poor girl,' Bill said sadly. 'Poor little thing. She had no idea how to look after herself, did she?'

'Evidently not since she's now lying on a slab in the pathology lab,' Nick said briskly, before the conversation became too maudlin. 'You take a quick look upstairs, I'll scout round down here.'

Bill duly disappeared upstairs. Instead of poking round, Nick sat down and drank in the stale atmosphere. No wonder Frisco had spent so much time out on the moors. She had not so much slipped through the welfare safety net as cut her way calmly through it, leaving it in ribbons. He, Nick Trevellyan, had let her down, failed to warn her against strange men. He had subscribed to the Mind-Your-Own-Business fallacy and passed by on the other side of the road. The animosity which he always felt towards murderers had become personal. He heard Bill coming back down.

'I'm going to get you for this,' he said quietly. 'Whoever you are. She was happy and carefree and she never did you any harm.'

'Nothing up there,' Bill said. 'I don't think she really used that part of the house. She obviously slept down here and there's no bathroom up there.' Bill peered out of the filthy kitchen window. 'No, look there's an outdoor toilet at the bottom of the garden.'

'I didn't really expect to find anything,' Nick said with a sigh. 'Let's get back to the station and see if we can find something edible in the canteen.'

'Miss Hope not back yet?'

'Not yet.'

Bill looked at him with sympathy. The inspector usually got a bit snappy when Miss Hope was away but this time he seemed very low in spirits. It was unnatural for a woman to go off galavanting all the time, leaving her man at home.

They locked up carefully, more from force of habit than any fear that Frisco's meagre belongings might be in jeopardy. They stood in Church Path for a moment in the beginnings of a drizzle, looking along the ill-assorted collection of cottages. There were nine of them in three groups of three, all backing on to the graveyard—their rear gardens funereal with laurel. Dot Lawson's cottage, with its cheerful yellow door and hanging basket, was neat and cared-for. Two others were prosperous enough, their pink-stoned fronts festooned with honeysuckle, clematis and climbing roses. Two stood empty. The rest, including the three owned by Frisco, looked poor and unloved with missing slates and dirty windows and overgrown vegetation.

'I dunno though,' Bill said. 'There's some cottages like this up in Hopwood. Three of them got sold the other day to some townies—gonna knock them into one big place.' He snorted in disgust. 'Just for weekends, like. I ask you. Fifty thousand they paid for them and they're in no better condition than these.'

'How do you know all this?' Nick asked.

'The estate agent's wife told Susie at the WI.' The WI, via Susie Deacon, was one of Bill's major sources of information. Very reliable they were too—keeping their ears to the ground better than any snout.

'I hope the valley's not going to become fashionable,' Nick said xenophobically. 'Fifty thousand. That would sound like a lot of money to some people.'

'It sounds like a lot of money to me,' Bill said. 'Here, you remember that place just up the valley where that blonde divorcee lived, the one that got burgled a couple of years back? That was the same sort of thing only all poshed up.'

'Mrs Sullivan,' Nick said with a smile. He had memories of Anne Sullivan of which Bill knew nothing.

'That's her. The one you had a bit of a thing with,' Bill said, ruthlessly shattering Nick's illusions. Nick cleared his throat. 'She sold that place for a small fortune.'

Nick turned his collar up and dived along the gloomy alleyway and back into the police car as the rain began to beat down relentlessly. Bill got into the driver's seat, started the car and turned it back towards Hopbridge.

'It's bloody raining again,' he said, trained never to overlook the obvious.

'What did you make of *Twelfth Night* then?' Nick asked, to take his mind off his own troubles.

'I quite enjoyed it funnily enough. I see what you meant about that Malvolio character. You always like to see people like that taken down a peg or two, don't you?'

Nick looked at the wet landscape and sighed.

'The rain it raineth every day,' he said.

IT WASN'T RAINING in West London and Alison was sitting on the terrace of Janine Baxter's house, looking out over the park to the spires of Brentford on the horizon. Beyond the garden wall a midweek football match was taking place to occasional shouts of joy, disapprobation and speculations on the players' parentage from the crowd of four spectators and a small mongrel.

Alison took a long sip of her white wine and Perrier and snuggled down more comfortable in her deckchair. Jan lit a cigarette and put the spent match carefully back in the box. Alison screamed silently.

'So you finally left that software house?' she asked.

'Yes.' Jan shuddered. 'Never again.'

'How long a break are you going to take this time?'

'About a year.'

'Can you afford it?'

'Yes. But the question is academic. I have to take about a year off.'

'What are you on about?' Alison asked affectionately. 'Peter's not whisking you off to New York for a year again, is he? That was another occasion on which you said "never again", as I recall.'

'You can be very dense sometimes, Alison. I'm expecting a baby in six months' time.' Alison stared at her open-mouthed. 'Do take that dumb look off your face,' Jan said crossly. 'It has been known, you know. I'm not the first woman ever to think of it.'

'I just thought, after all these years you and Peter have been together, that if you wanted children you would have had them before now. Was it planned?'

Jan laughed ironically. 'This is one of the most planned children in the history of the world. It has taken us three years to achieve.'

'Oh. I had no idea.'

'You cannot imagine the happy hours we have both spent waiting in hospitals to take endless humiliating tests, apparently to no avail. Until now. I was begin-

ning to think I'd have to do what the farmer does when
the hens stop laying.'

'What's that?' Alison asked.

'Change the cock, of course.'

Alison groaned. 'Should you be smoking?'

'Oh, do shut up. More wine?'

'Just a little. I'm driving back soon.'

Jan got up, fetched the wine from the fridge and
topped up Alison's glass. Then she stood up on the
narrow parapet of the terrace to give herself a view over
the wall at the football match. The captain of one team
was shouting, 'Move out! Move out!'

'Preferably to another park,' Jan said.

'Be careful,' Alison said nervously.

'Don't be silly. You can be godmother if you like.
Might as well give the little brat a nice, rich godmother.' They both fell silent for a few minutes as, over
their heads, Concorde began its descent into Heath-
row, making civilised conversation temporarily impossible. Jan sat down again and put her feet up on the
parapet. When the noise had died away she said, 'Are
you staying for supper, Alison?'

'No thanks. I want to get home.'

'Something tastier waiting for you there?'

'I hope so,' Alison said quietly. 'Can I use your
phone?'

NICK SAT IN HIS OFFICE considering his next move. He
had given a brief statement to some reporters about the
murder that Tuesday and the story was beginning to
appear in the local papers. The valley no longer had its
own newspaper but the story would be covered by the
county ones. There had been no recent pictures of

Frisco but the school had dug up a class photo of five years ago and that had been blown up and given to the newsmen. There had been a bit about it in the nationals too, though murders of young girls had become so frequent as to be barely news any more. It would take a serial murderer to get much national coverage. God forbid that it should come to that.

He remembered what Bill had said about tracing her mother. He made a few phone calls to other police forces starting with the Metropolitan force but no one had any records of an Iris Carstairs. It might be necessary to make an appeal on television for her mother to come forward. At least she could sort out Frisco's affairs.

Mike Brewster popped in during the afternoon to report that Ben Lawson had group O blood but was not a secretor.

'Sorry to disappoint,' he said, helping himself to one of the absent Bill's digestive biscuits.

'On the whole, I'm very glad to hear it,' Nick said.

Later that afternoon Nick drove out to Little Hopford and turned his car into the still dark and silent Hope Cottage. As he let himself in and switched off the burglar alarm, he realised that the answering machine was engaged in some masturbatory antic and he eyed this barrier to respectable human communication with annoyance as the incoming tape began to whirr.

He picked up the receiver quietly and held it to his ear.

'Hello, it's me,' Alison was saying in the special voice people reserve for answering machines. 'It's Thursday afternoon. I shall be back tonight—about eight if there

are no hold-ups. If you're there, Nick, I hope I'll see
you then. I . . . um . . . Message end.'

'Oh, I'll be here,' Nick said and hung up, grinning
as he imagined Alison's face.

TEN

AFTER SUPPER they sat in front of the log fire, on the sofa. Nick was at one end, reading one of the local papers which had rather a bad picture of himself in it. Alison was propped against the other arm with her feet on his lap, finishing a detective story she had bought in London.

Alison reached the last page of her book, groaned and threw it across the room.

'If I read another whodunnit where the policeman did it, I'm going to throw up. It's a good job you were in Venice with me when Frisco was murdered. Mind you, Bill Deacon and Reg Grey were here, you don't think—'

'No,' Nick said firmly, 'I don't. Bill Deacon's the most decent man I know. Anyway, what possible motive could he have?'

'He's married, isn't he? Perhaps he was one of Frisco's visitors and she threatened to tell Susie. The Superintendent now—'

'He's not married. His wife left him years ago.'

'He's got his reputation to think of though.'

'Yes, Frisco would qualify as associating with undesirables.'

'What?'

'Nothing.'

'So it might be him. It could be any man with a wife, or a position to protect.'

'Yes,' Nick said thoughtfully, 'or both. Pass the phone, will you.'

'Who are you calling?' she asked, passing the cordless handset over.

'I thought I'd give Lucy Fielding a ring.'

'You don't imagine Frisco did O level French, I suppose?' Alison said rather sharply.

'No.' Nick tapped in the number. 'But Lucy takes an interest in people. She may be able to tell me something about Frisco, and she'll certainly know a bit about Alan Lawson. Come on. Answer the phone... No reply.' He glanced at his watch. 'Out at one of her interminable meetings.'

'Or she might have gone away for the holidays. School doesn't start again until Monday.'

'True, I'll try tomorrow morning, though.' Nick put his paper down and began to caress her feet.

'I stopped off for tea at Jan's on the way home,' she said.

'How is she?'

'Pregnant!' Alison managed to look vaguely bewildered as if uncertain how this might happen.

'Really? Do give her my best wishes when next you speak to her.'

'OK. Apparently they've been trying for three years. It's ironic, isn't it? When you think how easily girls like Frisco get pregnant.'

'Frisco was more than ten years younger, of course. Are she and Peter going to get married?'

'Eh? They've been married for years. I was her bridesmaid. It must have been ... seven years ago.'

'Oh? I just assumed, as they had different surnames—'

'How old-fashioned you are. Jan didn't change her name when she got married.'

'That's one woman in the world who can be tracked down then,' Nick said. Alison, who was used to his obscure remarks, took no notice. 'Are you going to take my name when we get married?' he asked with malice aforethought. He licked her big toe.

'You mean "if" rather than "when", don't you?'

'Aha! Not completely out of the question then?'

'Don't use your CID interrogation techniques on me,' Alison said, withdrawing foot privileges.

'I couldn't resist it . . . Alison?'

'Mmm?'

'Do you want to have children?'

'Yes, I suppose so. One day. In a few years.'

'With me?'

'Certainly with you. What sort of question is that?'

'Just checking.'

NICK RANG LUCY'S NUMBER at half-past nine the next morning.

'It's Nick,' he said when she answered, 'Nick Trevellyan.'

'How many Nicks do you think I know? It's nice to hear from you. Business or pleasure?'

'Business. I wondered if you could tell me something about Alan Lawson.'

'Oh him,' she said in disgust. 'What about him?'

'You don't like him, I take it.'

'No, do you?'

'I'm not allowed to have personal opinions about people.' Lucy made a derisive noise. 'What's wrong with him?'

'He's...clammy. He looks at me and I know he wants to touch me up with his clammy little hands but he's too spineless even to try.'

'Odd that he got to be the youngest deputy head in the county then, if he's so awful,' Nick remarked.

'Oh, his awfulness isn't obvious—it takes a trained eye. I'm something of a connoisseur of male sexuality. Don't you remember?'

'Stop flirting, or I shall hang up.'

'I feel sorry for Angela,' she said, ignoring him. 'Of course she's not my sort at all, so very what-will-the-neighbours-say. But all the same, being married to him...' She added a few coarse speculations about the Lawsons' sex life in general and Alan Lawson's anatomy in particular which made Nick chuckle.

'What's all this about, anyway?' she said, suddenly suspicious. 'Has he been flashing in Riverside Park?'

'I'm investigating the Carstairs murder.'

'Of course, how stupid of me. Poor kid.'

'Did you know her?'

'Just to speak to, I never taught her. She wasn't exactly exam material. Where does Alan come in?'

'I don't know. Nowhere probably. I just wondered if you could help.'

'He was her form tutor, I think, when she was in the fourth form. What sort of thing do you want to know?'

'The last thing I want to do is put words in your mouth, Lucy, or ideas in your head. I just wondered what you thought of him, that's all.'

The pause was a lengthy one. Nick waited patiently. Lucy didn't have much time for the police and the chances were she would tell him to go to hell. He spent the hiatus trying to make pictures out of the twenty-three cracks on his office ceiling. There was definitely a little mountain in the corner with the cobweb above it acting as cloud cover.

When Lucy spoke again it was to say: 'It's awful what happened to Frisco. I'd like to help. If you mean did he give her any of those clammy looks, the answer is yes.'

'I see. But maybe he does that to all the young girls.'

'No, just the odd one or two.'

'Any suspicion that it might have gone beyond a look?'

'Nick, I'm just speculating. I can't say any more. I don't know anything.'

'OK, Lucy. Thanks very much for your help.'

'You can buy me a drink sometime.'

'Yes, sure,' he said uncertainly. 'Sometime.'

'Oh, I get it. Alison has got you on a tight leash.'

'That's the first time I've ever heard you make a bitchy remark, Lucy. It was unworthy of you.'

Lucy's reply was succinct. 'Balls!'

'See you. I certainly owe you that drink.' He hung up.

Nick sat thinking for a while, drumming his pen monotonously on the table. Then he looked out Alan Lawson's number and rang it.

'Mrs Lawson? Detective Inspector Trevellyan here. I'd like to talk to your husband again. Today please, as it's still the school holidays.'

'Yes,' Angela said. 'There is something my husband wants to talk to you about.'

Her manner towards him had changed subtly. He was no longer a double glazing salesman, but at least an assistant bank manager. When people started being polite to him it always set his antennae quivering.

'You'd better come round at once and get it over with,' Angela said abruptly and rang off.

NICK AND BILL reached the Lawsons' house at about half-past ten. Angela opened the door again, showing them into the sitting room this time. Alan Lawson was already there. He was nervous. He was fidgeting.

Angela said quite gently, 'You must tell them, Alan.' Alan swallowed painfully.

'Just a minute,' Nick said. 'I have to caution you first.'

'I'm not confessing to anything,' Alan said in anguish. 'I didn't kill her.'

'But if you have something to tell me concerning the case, I'm going to caution you anyway.' He did so.

'It doesn't concern the case, the murder I mean,' Alan insisted. 'I didn't tell you the whole truth the other day, about Frisco. I knew her better than I implied, a lot better.' He hesitated. 'Is it true what they said at the inquest—that she was pregnant?'

'Of course it's true,' Angela said tartly. 'Why would the police tell lies at inquests? Get on with it.'

'Were you the father of her child, Mr Lawson, is that it?' Nick asked.

'No! It wasn't mine, I swear it. But...' He looked round the room in panic. 'I did have sex with her once—not once, more than once.'

'I see.' What a surprise. 'When was this?'

'Ages and ages ago, when she was at the school. It must have been four years ago. At least.'

'When she was fifteen? Under age and in your "pastoral" care?' Nick said evenly. Alan's tone was instantly one of whining self-justification.

'I was a fourth-form tutor that year. She was in my class. I knew about her, of course. She seemed to make a beeline for me from the start. It was all right at first. I just laughed it off, took care never to be alone in the classroom with her. But then in the spring, Angela had been in hospital having our first. She'd had a hard time of it. It put her off for ages afterwards... you know. Frisco knew or guessed what I was going through. She took advantage of me.'

Bill Deacon gave a snort of disgust as the memory of Frisco's lifeless body floated into his mind's eye.

'I know what you're thinking but it's true,' Alan said desperately. 'You don't know what she was like. I didn't have a chance.'

'How long did this affair go on?' Nick asked.

'About four weeks.'

'You told your wife about this? At the time?'

'No, not until yesterday. She knew nothing about it.'

'Where did you go to meet Miss Carstairs?'

'Threeoaks Hill, in the copse. I was terrified, I thought someone would come by.' He licked his dry lips. 'Then Angela was getting better and I put a stop to it. I told her I wouldn't see her again. She took it well enough. She wasn't the sort to make a fuss. She'd had her fun.'

'Very convenient, sir,' Bill said.

Nick said, 'And what about the next time?'

Alan looked round at his wife. She said quietly, 'Tell them everything, Alan.'

'I ran into her in Hopbridge two years later. She'd left school by then, of course, and I'd heard that she was living alone in Little Hopford. Angela was pregnant with our little girl. It... well, it just started up again.' Nick was silent and Alan rushed on, the words tumbling out in guilty torrents.

'I went to her cottage once, but it was an awful squalid place and she didn't seem to like me going there. Said something about her grandmother not liking it. I didn't understand that—I thought the old woman was dead. And Mum might have seen us. So we went up to the copse again. I saw her a few times but then I broke with her and I haven't seen her since. If she was pregnant it certainly wasn't mine.'

'Have you seen her recently—just to speak to, for example?' Nick glanced at Angela, now pregnant again—a state which seemed to have an unfortunate effect on her husband. She looked back steadily; reading his thoughts; rejecting his tacit sympathy; despising him for feeling it.

'I saw her in the street a couple of weeks ago. I bought her a drink for old times' sake. She said she'd met someone she could really be happy with. I was pleased for her. I didn't realise she meant Ben.'

'So when you heard she was engaged to him that evening in the pub?'

'I was thunderstruck. I would never have allowed it to happen. Even if it meant the whole truth coming out.'

'Did you see her on Sunday night?'

'No, no.'

'Where were you between seven and nine that evening?' Nick asked.

'Was that when it happened? I went to the golf club at opening time and had a few drinks there. I was there until about half-past nine. Ask anyone.'

'What time did you get home.'

'About . . .' He looked at his wife. 'About eleven.'

'And how do you account for the gap, Mr Lawson?'

'I went for a walk, to think about Ben and Frisco. Trying to make up my mind if... and how much... I should tell Angela.'

'Miss Carstairs died between ten and twelve, sir,' Nick said quietly. Alan winced. 'Where did your walk take you?'

'Just across the golf course. It's quiet there at night.'

'See anyone? Or, more to the point, did anyone see you?'

'No,' Alan said miserably. 'I didn't see a soul. But I didn't go to Threeoaks Hill. I didn't kill her.'

'I'd like you to come down to the station with us,' Nick said. 'I want you to provide a blood sample and a sperm sample. If it wasn't you with her that night then tests will help to prove it.' Alan stared at him in speechless horror.

'Are you arresting him?' Angela asked calmly.

'Not if he's prepared to co-operate. If not, then I shall.'

'I don't know anything about it,' Alan said. 'I don't see how you can arrest me.'

Nick was getting very sick of Alan Lawson. 'Let's start with illegal intercourse with an under-age girl, shall we?' he said. 'An indictable offence to which you have just confessed. I'll need a warrant to arrest you for that. So I'll get one and come back this evening with a squad car and some uniformed constables. What time do the neighbours get home?'

'OK, OK, I'm coming.'

Bill was watching Alan Lawson in his rear view mirror as they drove to the station and Nick eyed him with trepidation. It was obvious that Bill, whose three daughters attended Hopbridge Comprehensive, was bursting to say something. If he threatened Alan with the school governors then Alan might think his career was finished anyway and stop co-operating. Nick disapproved of adultery as much as Bill did. Not on moral grounds but on the grounds that it was furtive and deceitful and emotionally messy and that one corner of the triangle, at least, was bound to get hurt. But this was not the time to remind Alan Lawson of his wedding vows. Nick managed to catch Bill's eye and gave a small shake of his head. Bill looked pained.

'He wasn't going to allow it to happen even if it meant telling the truth,' Bill said, when they had handed Alan over to Mike Brewster and were back in Nick's office. 'Or even if it meant getting the girl out of the way.' Bill had cast Alan as first murderer. 'The way I see it, sir, he had two possible motives. One, the kid was his, the girl was threatening to expose him. He took her up to the copse again that night and strangled her. Two, she was determined to marry his brother, he got her to meet him, couldn't dissuade her, raped her and strangled her.'

'She wasn't raped, Bill. There were no signs of force.'

'All right then, he gave her one for "old times' sake" then strangled her.'

'It's possible.' Nick said. 'Either of those theories is possible.'

'You'd think he'd have more sense, a man in his position, than to go messing about with little girls,' Bill said.

'Yes. And more sense than to admit to it too,' Nick said thoughtfully. He relied heavily on people admitting to things. He could never work out why they did it. There were a lot of people in jail who might well not be there if they'd just stuck to their stories. Or was Alan Lawson being very clever? Was he admitting to the lesser crime to obscure the greater? Had one angle of the triangle been not just hurt on this occasion, but killed?

'Mind you,' Bill said, breaking into Nick's reverie, 'I'm beginning to think the Lawson boy—the youngster, I mean—had a narrow escape. He was all set to make a right fool of himself over the girl, wasn't he?'

'It's one of those irregular verbs,' Nick said moodily.

'Eh?'

'I am in love. You are infatuated. He is making a fool of himself,' Nick elucidated. Bill looked at Nick as if he were mad which he did with increasing frequency in those days. Nick felt very tired.

By the time Alan Lawson got home that night, he was fighting hard to preserve his self-esteem.

'I don't know who Trevellyan thinks he is,' he said tightly. 'So bloody holier-than-thou. Everyone knows he was screwing Lucy Fielding, and now that stuck-up Hope woman. That rich bitch.'

'He's not married,' Angela said in a tired voice, 'and neither of them is under the age of consent.'

Alan didn't seem to hear her. 'Mind you,' he went on 'that tart, Lucy, she's not exactly unexplored territory. Luce, all her friends call her. Loose, is right.'

'Oh really!' Angela screamed. 'I bet she wouldn't give you the time of day though, would she, Alan?' She collapsed on a chair and began to sob, loudly, open-mouthed, uncaring. 'The baby is kicking, I'm exhausted, I wish it was me dead in that copse instead of her.'

Alan stared in horror, seeing his rock-like wife turn to quicksand beneath his feet. For the first time that week, indeed in many years, he was shaken out of his self-centred concern for number one.

'Angie?' he said hesitantly. He laid a hand on her shoulder but she twisted away from him in disgust. 'You don't think I killed her, do you? Not you. Please say you don't think so.'

'No, I don't think so,' Angela choked out between sobs. 'You wouldn't have had to strangle her, Alan. You could just have bloody bored her to death.'

ELEVEN

'NICK, WAKE UP.'

'Lucy? Sorry, I was miles away.'

'So I observed.' She sat down opposite him at the table. 'I thought I'd find you here, your second home.'

'Very funny.'

'I know people leave messages for you here.'

'I shall treat that remark with the contempt it deserves,' Nick said, getting up. 'This seems the ideal time to buy you that drink. Red wine?'

'Half a bitter, please.'

'Cheapest information I've bought in a long time. Want to sign on as one of my regular snouts?' He brought her beer, she took a sip of it, yawned and sighed. 'You look tired,' he said.

'Gee, thanks. You look terrible, Lucy. You're thirty-seven and your looks are beginning to go.'

'You look terrific and you know it. Just today, you happen to look tired, as if you hadn't been sleeping lately.'

'The Easter holidays are too damn short. Oh well, at least in the summer term there are exams and I only have to teach half my classes.'

'I thought you liked teaching.'

'You like being a fascist copper but that doesn't stop you moaning when they phone you up in the middle of the night or when you're eating your dinner.' The pub was almost empty but Lucy, who could spot a bourgeois in need of *épatement* at a hundred paces, raised her voice. 'Or on the job.'

A pair of elderly ladies began to talk loudly and simultaneously over their half pints of milk stout. Nick smiled and said unconcernedly: 'Go and wash your mouth out with carbolic.'

Lucy peered into her glass. 'I think this will do just as well.' She took another sip of it anyway and said more quietly, 'Have you arrested Alan then?'

'No.'

'Did he kill her?'

'I'm inclined to think not. He's pretty reprehensible but I don't see him as a murderer. He's just what you said—spineless. Bill on the other hand wants to lock him up and mislay the key.'

'Was he screwing Frisco?'

'You must know I can't tell you that.'

'What if he was? That's his and her business.'

'She was under age!'

'So he was screwing her, I thought so.'

'Lucy! You tricked that out of me.'

'Well, you'll have to do better than that, Nick. Don't worry, I'm not going to gossip about it. I shall just smile sweetly at him next time he makes a snide remark to me—and let him wonder how much I know. How useful to have a friend who's a policeman. Or an ex-friend.'

'You're in a funny mood today. I thought we were friends.'

'Alison Hope permitting. Does she know about me?'

'Yes, of course.'

'Oh. What did you tell her? That I was just a black tart you used to hang around with? Before you moved into a higher league—designer dresses and flash cars?'

Nick looked at her thoughtfully for a moment. 'That remark sounded suspiciously racist and sexist,' he said finally. 'And I don't own a single designer dress.'

'What does it take to get a rise out of you?'

'Why do you want to?'

'Why do you always answer questions with another question?'

'What's wrong with that?'

'Even when you came home that day and found me in bed with Bob, in *your* bed, you didn't lose your temper.'

'Is that why you did it? I did wonder sometimes. When I hadn't anything better to think about.'

'Aha! A hint of bitchiness at last. Something human.'

'May we call a halt to this game, Lucy? I haven't had time to study the rules. If you won't tell me what's biting you then let's talk about the weather.'

'I'm sorry, Nick. Will anything happen to Alan, about the under-age bit, I mean?'

'I shouldn't think so for a moment. I'm looking for a murderer not a pathetic nymphophile.'

'But you seem to think it's an offence.'

'It's not a matter of opinion. It *is* an offence. But the Crown Prosecution Service will never prosecute now. It was several years ago.'

'And besides the wench is dead? I suppose I'm glad really. What with the two little kids and another on the way. I must be turning *bourgeoise*.'

'Horribly.'

'You know Max Bannister has been arrested?'

'Uh huh. I told you a long time ago he was a drug addict and would soon start pushing.'

'And I didn't believe you, I know. He's out on bail now. What will he get?'

'I don't know. But I gather he will be giving evidence for the prosecution so he may get off quite lightly.'

'Max!'

'Didn't you know? They're still missing a few links in the chain that led up to London. They're hoping Bannister will solder the chain for them.' They were clutching at straws. Bannister was a very small link indeed. They might have to reconcile themselves to the many who got away—this time.

'Max would never do that,' Lucy was saying.

'Don't you believe it. When it's a question of saving his own skin—principle soon takes a jump out of the window.'

'Cynical, aren't you?' Lucy said coldly.

'When it comes to druggies? Horribly. Do you know what they all say in the interview room?'

'Who?'

'Drug pushers. They all say, "If I didn't do it, someone else would." Public benefactors, every last one of them, supplying a need rather than creating it. Except that they hang around outside schools, waiting for *your* pupils, Lucy, handing out a few freebies to get them hooked. Then it's theft, mugging and prostitution—the boys too—anything to fund the habit. "If it wasn't me it would be someone else!"'

'Sometimes I think you're not just a fascist who likes bullying people. Sometimes I think you care.'

'Yeah? I must be slipping.'

They sat in silence for a moment then Nick said, 'You know Angela Lawson a bit. Will she leave Alan?'

'I doubt it. I don't suppose she had any illusions about him anyway, not after six years. Doesn't mean she won't make him suffer for it though. He has sinned against the great god, Fidelity. Fidelity! I don't think it matters.'

'No, so I recall. But I do.'

She looked at him seriously for a moment then said unexpectedly, 'Suppose we had still been living together when you met Alison.'

'We weren't really living together,' Nick said cautiously.

'More or less.'

'You still kept on your own flat.'

'Oh yeah? Rumour has it that you've still got your own flat, even though you're living with Alison.'

'*Touché*. Suppose we were. So?'

'So! Then suppose you'd met Alison and fallen for her. What price fidelity then?'

'I honestly don't know the answer to that question, Lucy.'

'Don't you? I do.'

'Hello there, you two.' Alison sat down on the empty chair between them.

Lucy had never believed all that stuff you read in books about people's eyes lighting up, particularly when it came to this most inscrutable of men. The nearest she had seen to it with Nick had been on the evening they had met, three years before. The lights had come on as *Providence* flickered to an end at the French Film Club and she had noticed him for the first time as he took off his glasses to rub his eyes. She had gone over and said, 'Hello. You're new, aren't you?' and for a second, as he glanced up, desire had darted into his eyes and been so swiftly expelled that she had wondered, until later that night, if she had imagined it. He never looked at her that way now.

After a few seconds he reached his hand across the table and took Alison's as though he could not bear a second longer not to touch her. All this served only to aggravate the heavy, thundery depression which had been building up in Lucy's head for the past twenty-four hours. She was about to make her excuses and leave when it occurred to her that that would simply confirm any suspicions Alison might be harbouring. She didn't care what Alison thought but she did care about hurting Nick. She stayed put.

'Your desk sergeant said I'd find you in here,' Alison was saying. '"Mr Trevellyan will be in the Bird and Baby, Miss." Fine reputation you've got.'

'The uniformed boys get disappointed if CID don't spend all their time in the pub,' Nick explained.

'What? Drinking tomato juice?'

'I pass it off as a Bloody Mary. You've met Lucy Fielding, haven't you?'

'Yes, of course. Hello, Lucy.' Lucy nodded a greeting.

'People leave messages here for him,' she said.

'That's not true,' Nick said loftily. 'Do you want a drink, Alison?'

'My round, I think. Lucy? Same again?'

'Er, well,' Lucy said, looking dubiously into her glass but Alison had already turned round in her chair and was hailing the barman.

'Chris?'

'Yes? Oh hello, Alison.'

'Can I have a half of bitter, another Virgin Mary, a G and T for me, and whatever you're having.'

'Thanks, coming right up.'

'Bring them over to the table, will you?'

'OK, seeing as it's you.'

'I never knew such a woman for not putting herself to any trouble,' Nick said, in mock admiration.

'He's standing up already,' Alison explained. 'It's a questions of ergonomics.'

'What brings you into town, anyway?'

'Dot didn't turn up this morning. Didn't ring or anything. The house is such a tip, I couldn't stand it a moment longer.'

'Oh dear. I'm afraid I upset her by questioning her two chicks.'

'Yes, I thought somehow it must be your fault. I suppose I shall have to grovel to get her back.' Nick adopted a look of strained disbelief. 'And you can take that look of strained disbelief off your face,' Alison said.

'Can I watch?' was all Nick said.

'Solved your case yet?' Alison asked acidly.

'No.'

'Shouldn't you be off pulling someone's fingernails out then instead of skulking in the pub?'

'I came in here for a quiet think, out of reach of my telephone, but people keep interrupting me.'

Lucy caught Alison's eye and smiled glumly. 'I think that was a subtle hint,' she said.

'Thanks, Chris. Here.' Alison handed the barman a five pound note. 'I was going to offer to buy you lunch, Nick.'

'That would have been nice, my angel, but I have got to go and talk to someone as it happens. It occurred to me just before I bumped into Lucy.'

'What about you, Lucy?'

'Eh?' Lucy said in amazement.

'Can I buy you lunch, at the Pheasant?'

'Er... yeah... OK. Thanks,' said Lucy, caught out without a clean excuse.

'Drink up then, I'm starving. We'll leave Lord Peter Wimsey to his thinking.'

A phone rang in the back room and the barman went to answer it. He came back after a moment and called loudly across the bar.

'Message for you, Nick, Can you get back to your office right away?'

Lucy and Alison laughed at the look on Nick's face. Nick strolled back to the station at a leisurely pace. Whatever it was couldn't be *that* urgent. He wasn't sure he liked the idea of Alison and Lucy having lunch together. They might talk about him, or was that just paranoia? They would both no doubt say that they had better things to talk about. He didn't see how they could get on—Alison being such a capitalist fat cat while Lucy had her knitting ready for sitting under the guillotine. He reached the station and found Bill waiting for him at the foot of the stairs.

'Don't leave messages for me at the pub,' Nick said reproachfully.

'Sorry, sir. Couple of things. Doc Brewster rang through to say that Lawson, Alan Lawson that is, is blood group AB.'

'Is he now? That puts him in the clear as well then.'

'Yeah,' Bill said unhappily. 'Shame.'

'Cheer up.' Nick clapped his old friend on the shoulder. 'It only proves it wasn't he who had sex with her that night. He could still be the murderer.' Bill looked happier. 'What was the other thing?'

'Miss Carstairs' mother has turned up—that was why I thought I'd better track you down, urgent like. I've put her in your office.'

'Well, well. Let's take a look at this advertisement for the maternal instinct, shall we?'

Nick took the stairs to the second floor two at a time with Bill lumbering behind.

Iris Paignton was a hard-faced woman in her early forties. She looked like the landlady of a prosperous pub—with a professionally hovering smile and a brewery-supplied air of good-natured competence. She had not felt the need to sober up her dress for the occasion. Her make up was far from discreet. Nick had a subconscious conviction that heavily-powdered women were wearing some sort of mask and, it followed logically, hiding something.

Her manner was businesslike, her accent London. Nick felt obliged to offer his condolences although they seemed superfluous in view of the fact that Iris Carstairs had abandoned her daughter at the age of two. He looked in vain for some echo of Frisco's carefree grace in this tightly encased figure.

'I came as soon as I heard,' she was saying briskly. 'But I can't stay long. I've got a pub to run.' Full marks to Lord Peter Wimsey.

'It won't take long,' he said. 'The body has been formally identified. Unless you've been in touch with your daughter during the last couple of years I don't think you can be of much help in our enquiries.'

'Good. I just want to get things cleared up, get her buried and sell those awful cottages.'

'The coroner has released the body for burial.' Nick suppressed his instinctive dislike of the woman. After all Frisco had been no more than a stranger to her. 'When did you last see or hear from your daughter?'

'I didn't. I mean not since I left eighteen years ago. Mum wrote to me at first but we were neither of us great letter writers and then I was moving around a lot and we lost touch. I didn't even know she'd died until today—Mum, I mean. The last time I heard from her was about twelve years ago.'

'Can I have your address?' Nick asked. 'Your home address.'

'The Lynch Cross Arms, Allerford.' Nick looked at her in open surprise. She shrugged. 'Funny how you always drift back towards your home town, isn't it? However much you hate the bloody place.'

'I hadn't realised you lived locally.'

'I was up in London for fifteen years but then the old man had a hankering to run a country pub. We came down here.'

'But you didn't attempt to get in touch with your daughter—or your mother.'

'I'm not so vain as to imagine that either of them cared a damn about me after all these years.' She laughed without conviction. 'Blood thicker than water? Pull the other one.'

'Speaking of which, Mrs Paignton.' Nick hesitated, wondering how to phrase the question. 'Your daughter's father.'

'What about him? Who was he, you mean?'

'Well, yes.'

She shrugged. 'It was probably a yank who was stationed here for a year or two. I can't even remember his name, now. He went back to the States anyway, back to San Francisco. He didn't want to know.' She laughed again. 'He stumped up some cash for a backstreet but I didn't have the nerve. Mate of mine died that way—bled to death. Funny thing was they went and made it legal just when it was too late.'

Nick brought the conversation firmly back to the point. 'Probably a yank. So there was someone else,' he hesitated, choosing his words carefully, 'who might have had reason to think he was Frisco's father?'

She gave him a cool look. 'I was pretty certain.'

'What were you getting at?' Bill asked after she'd gone.

'I don't know really. It just occurred to me that some village man, now approaching middle age, might have thought . . . I don't know. Have we got Sam Lawson's records? Dig them out of the card index for me, will you. Sam was always a bit of a lady's man and he lived only a few doors away.'

Bill returned with the information. Nick glanced through it.

'The chances are that Sam was on one of his regular trips to Dartmoor or the Scrubs then—1966 to 7. No, he was out for eight months from September 1966 to April 1967. Must be some sort of record for him. Then he went back inside for two years. How interesting.'

'You mean if Sam Lawson thought he was her father, he'd go to some lengths to stop her marrying his son.'

'Perhaps, or on reflection perhaps it wouldn't bother him in the least. You can't always tell with the natives of this valley. In-breeding's almost as traditional as stag-hunting round here.'

'I'm a native of the valley,' Bill said coolly. 'And so are you.'

'Oh yes, I forgot. Exogamy rules, OK?'

'Mmmm,' said Bill who wanted to look exogamy up in a dictionary before committing himself further.

'It's a bit thin, but there's no point in sitting around here. We might as well be out doing something.'

'If it was that, he'd hardly have had sexual relations with her himself before killing her, would he?' Bill pointed out.

'No,' Nick said, crestfallen. 'It's too preposterous to think that the man she was with that evening isn't the man who killed her, isn't it? Still I think I'll have a little word with Sam all the same.' He glanced at his watch. 'This afternoon will be a good time. Dot will be out at Great Hopford doing her cleaning for the vicar.'

'You don't want her around when you talk to Sam?'

'I'd rather see him on his own. Dot's a much tougher prospect than he is.'

'You can say that again.'

'Meantime, get on to the police in Porlock and find out all you can about Mrs Paignton. Is Mr Paignton still in evidence? If not, who's the "old man" she referred to? Do they own that pub? Have they got any debts? Usual sort of thing.'

'You don't think—'

'I don't *think* anything. I just want some facts checked, OK?'

'Right, sir.'

'She looks like a woman who might kill someone for fifty thousand pounds. Don't you think?'

'If you say so, sir,' Bill said, meaning no.

'Do that now, then meet me back here at two-thirty and we'll pay that visit to Sam. I want to go out to the Hopfords anyway.'

'What for?'

'See if anyone knows the identity of an old man with a greyhound.'

TWELVE

'I HOPE YOU DIDN'T THINK...' Lucy said, when they were settled at their table and Alison was laying into a plate of whitebait as if she hadn't eaten for a fortnight. '...in the pub—me and Nick.'

'I didn't think anything of it,' Alison said, going slightly pink with the effort.

'He just rang me to ask about...someone I know.'

'Alan Lawson.'

'Yes. I suppose you would know all about it. I said he could buy me a drink sometime in return. So when I saw him there in the pub, on his own—'

'Honestly Lucy, I don't see you as any sort of threat.'

'Oh.'

'Now I've hurt your feelings! Are you always as prickly as this?'

'Don't patronise me, Alison Hope.'

Normally Alison would have risen to this challenge, but, sensing the other woman's pain, she put down her fork and said, 'Is there anything I can do?'

'Money can't buy everything.'

'I never imagined it could.'

'It can't raise the dead, Alison.'

'Who's dead?'

'My dad.'

'When?'

'A few days ago. I buried him yesterday.'

'Why didn't you tell me about it instead of screwing it up inside you?'

Lucy sat back in her chair and looked at Alison for
a moment. She was surprised to see genuine concern in
Alison's eyes and an unexpected warmth in the faint
curving smile of her lips. The dark alcoves of the
Pheasant's empty dining room brought back the con-
fessional of her Catholic girlhood. She came to a de-
cision.

'I spent all the Easter holidays up there, in Wolver-
hampton. They told me he was getting better. *He* told
me he was getting better. He persuaded me to come
home to get ready for the new term. Then they rang me
a few nights ago and told me he'd died. Peacefully.
Peacefully!'

'I know how you feel, Lucy.'

'It's so easy and glib to say that,' she said angrily.

'I do though. I remember when *my* father died, I felt
very helpless. His sheer resignation infuriated me. I
wanted to shake him…to shout at him, "Don't just sit
there taking it. Fight back, you bastard." Something
like that.'

Lucy smiled at last. 'Yes, that's exactly how I felt.'

'Did you tell Nick about it?'

'No. I don't want sympathy. Especially not his sympathy. He would have been so kind and understand-
ing. And I would have broken down. And howled. And
I didn't. Want. To do. That.'

Alison poured Lucy some more wine and pushed the
glass towards her. She took a gulp and almost choked.
Some minutes of spluttering and back-slapping en-
sued. The Portuguese waiter looked as if he might offer to rub Lucy's chest given half a chance. Alison
disposed of him with a look which made him curl up
round the edges like a week-old lettuce. Lucy resolved
to ask her how it was done, when she could speak

again. Then she reflected, spitefully, that you probably needed a long nose like Alison's and centuries of middle-class Anglo-Saxon breeding.

'I couldn't tell him,' she said when she'd got her voice back. 'That would have been the last straw.'

'You've told me.'

'Yeah.' Lucy's smile widened and moved up into her eyes. 'I knew I wouldn't get any sympathy from you...I feel better now. Thanks.'

Alison signalled the waiter back. 'Time for some more food and drink, especially more drink. Take the taste of that awful beer out of your mouth. I think they put the floor sweepings in it.'

They ate in silence for a while then Alison said, 'Is your mother dead too?'

'No. She divorced my father and went home to Martinique.'

'Only child?' Lucy shook her head.

'Two little brothers—twins, much younger. Maman took them with her. I cabled them when Dad was in the hospital but they didn't come. Didn't even reply.'

'I'm sorry.'

'Why is it so hard to trust the people you love most?' Lucy asked, redistributing her salmon around the plate without actually eating any of it.

Alison thought for a moment. 'Because if they let you down then there's no one left to turn to,' she said at last.

NICK AND BILL FOUND Sam Lawson at home as usual. He was alone.

'Dot all right?' Nick asked. 'Only Alison said she didn't come to Hope Cottage today.'

'None of my business what Dorothy does about her work,' Sam said surlily.

'Not working yourself?' Nick persevered.

'No. And I don't want your help to find a job either,' he said rudely. 'Now what d'you want? Social call, is it?'

'May we come in?'

Sam looked a bit surprised at being asked. 'Er, yeah, OK.' He led them through into the kitchen but made no further overtures of welcome. Nick sat down.

'I've just been having a chat with Iris Paignton,' he said. Sam looked blank. 'Iris Carstairs, that was.'

'Blimey! Don't tell me she's turned up to pick over the remains.'

'She is the girl's mother, and her heir.'

'Terrific mother she made.'

'You knew her pretty well from what she tells me.'

'What's that supposed to mean?'

'Well, she wasn't a hundred per cent sure who Frisco's father was, was she? I can see it was convenient to wish it on the yank—she probably thought he'd stump up more money. Especially with you being married already and not much of a provider at the best of times.'

Sam sat down, his eyes fixed on Nick. He'd never been much of a poker player. 'Big mouth Iris had,' he said at last. 'Big everything actually.'

'You knew Frisco might be yours.'

'She said so. I doubted it personally.'

'You were out of prison at the right time.'

'If you say so. I tend to lose track.'

'So what were you going to do about her and Ben?'

Sam stared at him. 'What about them?'

'Since you knew they might be half-brother and -sister.'

'You're the great detective. Can't you count? Since you've been snooping round my record.'

Bill glanced at his notes, then handed them to Nick.

'Out from September '66 to April '67,' Nick read. 'Then in Dartmoor until January 1969, breaking and entering—again.'

'That's right. And Ben was born in February 1969. Work it out for yourself, Mr Detective.'

Nick's mind raced into overdrive. Another father for Ben, another man who might have wanted to prevent a wedding.

'Do you know who Ben's father was?' he asked.

'Only what Dorothy told me.'

'So who did she say it was?'

Sam roared with laughter. Nick had never seen him so happy. His blue eyes twinkled with malice.

'Why, come to think of it, Ben's a relation of yours— Mr High-And-Mighty Trevellyan. A close relation.'

'I'M A COMPLETE IDIOT, Nick said that evening. 'It didn't even occur to me that Ben and Alan had different blood groups. All I was thinking about was that neither of them was the man with Frisco that night.'

'It could have been worse,' Alison said. 'He could have said it was your father.'

'I don't think so. You didn't know my dad. But Uncle Lynton? My face must have been a picture.'

'I wish I'd been a fly on the wall. Be fair though, Nick. Lynton was widowed quite young, wasn't he? And Dot had her bloke inside three-quarters of the time. They must both have got a bit lonely.'

'All the same. It was one of the most embarrassing moments of my life.'

'No wonder Dot's got that soft spot for you. You look a lot like Lynton, or a lot like he must have done twenty years ago.'

'I thought at first Sam was making it up but Dot got back soon after that and confirmed it. Mind you, I wouldn't have liked to be in Sam's shoes after we'd gone. She was furious with him. She did say one odd thing as she was seeing us out, though. She said she wouldn't trust Lynton further than the front door— and she was standing on the doorstep at the time.'

'Oh, well, people aren't always very objective about their former mates, are they?'

'No, I suppose not.'

'Speaking of which, we had a very good lunch at the Pheasant.'

'Oh yes. And what did you find to talk about?'

'We didn't talk about you, if that's what you mean. We had better things to discuss. We talked about murder in general and Frisco in particular. I invited her only out of some sort of weird perversity but I found I really liked her.'

'Why shouldn't you?' Nick wondered what Lucy had made of Alison who aroused many emotions but rarely indifference.

'Perhaps because of the way she looks at you under those dusky lids.' Nick blushed. Alison sat down on the sofa beside him. He put his arms round her and she nestled up against him.

'Did you find out what was biting her?' Nick asked.

'How d'you mean?' Alison stalled.

'Well, she was in a filthy temper in the pub this lunchtime.'

Alison shrugged. 'No, I've no idea.' She changed the subject. 'What were you and she talking about when I arrived?'

'I don't remember,' Nick said casually. He was an accomplished liar since his work often involved dissimulation—or, at the least, bluff. He believed in telling the truth outside work though, except where it was too inexpedient. Alison knew a lot about his relationship with Lucy—but not everything.

'You were saying you didn't know the answer to something and she said she did,' Alison prompted.

'We were just discussing the importance of fidelity in a relationship, apropos the Alan Lawsons.'

'I think it's very important.'

'Good, so do I. Thanks for not making a scene in the pub.'

'Well, I considered it but as you were sitting at opposite ends of the table, I thought I'd just make myself look stupid. But I'll tell you now, and get it over with, that if you're ever unfaithful to me it will be all over between us. I'm not a doormat like Angela Lawson.'

'Neither is Angela Lawson actually.'

'Did she kill Frisco? You've only got her word for it that she didn't know about the affair.'

'I have thought about it. It's hard to imagine a more unattractive picture than that of a heavily pregnant woman creeping about Threeoaks Hill late at night to strangle another pregnant woman. And I don't see how she could have known Frisco was pregnant—no one knew for sure—so why wait until now? Why not kill her years ago?'

'She might only just have found out about the affair, a week or two ago. Or perhaps she found out quite a while ago but only started brooding about it now she's pregnant again—thinking Alan would go off the rails for a third time.'

'I doubt if she's got the physical strength. Frisco was a frail little thing but you'd still need considerable strength to kill her so quickly that she hardly had time to struggle. Strangling is really a man's crime, unless the victim is a child, say.'

'It seems odd that Frisco wasn't sleeping with Ben,' Alison said, her fertile mind wandering off in another direction. 'It implies . . .'

'Yes? Go on. I need all the help I can get.'

'That there was someone else . . . someone really important to her, I mean.'

'Possible. It's possible. The man who was with her that night, the father of her child.'

'And she must have met him during the last four months. Since Christmas, say.'

'How come?'

'Because she was still up to her usual tricks with Jake just before Christmas.'

'Good thinking. Thanks.'

'What a puzzle she is, was.' Alison thought for a moment then said, 'Hercule Poirot once said that the reason for a murder is nearly always to be found by a study of the person murdered.' Alison had been reading Agatha Christie for inspiration for her computer game and Nick was getting a bit tired of Poirot's *bons mots*. He decided to put him in his place.

'Hercule Poirot is a fictional character. Ouch! That hurt, Alison.' He sighed. 'Let's forget about it for tonight, shall we? I can come to it with a clear mind in the morning. What's on the telly?' He used the remote control to flick round the channels and came up with a detective serial set in Newcastle and featuring a very fit young detective sergeant who was always running after criminals and rugby tackling them to the ground.

'Just the thing, a bit of escapism,' he said.

In his spare time the detective practised martial arts with a colleague. In the evening he was in bed with a girl.

'Pillow talk,' Nick said priggishly. 'Not allowed.'

'What do you mean?'

'A policeman is not supposed to tell his wife or girlfriend about his cases.'

'Since when?'

'Since always.'

'You're always telling me things. What have we just been talking about?'

'Shh,' Nick said in a serious tone. 'Reg Grey may be outside the front door, at this very moment, listening to every word.'

The doorbell rang insistently.

'I'll go,' Nick said, when he had recovered his *sang froid*.

'Good idea,' Alison said. 'After all there is a possibly crazed killer on the loose in the valley.'

Nick considered this. 'Perhaps we might use the entry phone.' Alison had already picked it up. An impatient voice squawked through it.

'Alison, is that you? It's Ralph. Can I come in?'

By the time the front door opened Nick was safely upstairs in the study watching the end of the serial on the portable TV. When the serial finished he watched the *News at Ten* as well. Then he put his head out of the door and listened. Ralph was obviously still there. In fact he was quite certain to stay the night. He would have to go down and be polite. He sighed, went down the stairs and entered the drawing room.

'Hello,' he said.

'Um, Mick, isn't it?' Ralph said, already into his third malt whisky.

'Very nearly, Rolf.'

The two men eyed each other with ill-concealed distaste. Ralph found it hard to reconcile the five foot ten of undoubted masculinity that was Nick with his cherished idea that Alison still carried a torch for him and, although Alison had assured him that she and Ralph had never been lovers, Nick was only ninety-nine per cent certain that he believed her. Even if Ralph had been her lover, Nick could hardly object to his presence, since Alison had caught him *in flagrante delicto* in the pub with Lucy that very lunchtime. Damn, damn, damn.

'Staying with us long, Ralph?' he enquired politely, partly to emphasize the "us" and partly hoping for the answer no.

'Thought I'd combine business with pleasure and spend a good few days down here picking up some antiques,' Ralph said, dashing Nick's hopes.

Alison came in with the coffee tray and, sizing up the situation, was preparing to call them both to order when Nick said, 'Antiques? Always a good cover for stolen goods.'

'Nick!' she protested.

'Sorry, my angel, just thinking aloud.'

The corners of his mouth twitched as he tried not to laugh at the expression on Ralph's face.

THIRTEEN

'ARE YOU SURE you want to sell this bureau, Molly?' Alison asked. 'I thought it had been in your family for generations.'

'Not exactly. It belonged to my godmother, Mary Stephenson. She was quite the worst kind of repressed spinster. I always hated having to go to stay with her. I've always hated her bureau too but never had the nerve to get rid of it—I was afraid she would come back and haunt me. But every time I look at it, I see her pinched old face looking disapproving. She always disapproved—it didn't matter what it was. So when you told me about Ralph, here, I took it as a sign. I believe there's quite a market for them.'

'Yes, some,' Ralph said non-comittally. 'It's awfully big, of course, so that limits the market a bit. You'd need a big house with good-sized rooms—somewhere like Hope Cottage, for example.'

'If I thought Alison wanted it,' Molly said repressively, 'I would hardly need you as a middle man. But I wouldn't wish it on her.'

'It's in lovely condition,' Alison said. 'What is it? Walnut?'

'No,' Ralph said scornfully. 'Mahogany. The fact is, Molly, that I'm not sure how much to offer you. It's an unusual piece, Can I have a think about it?'

'Yes, of course. But you are interested?'

'Definitely. I'd certainly like first refusal.'

'Get it properly valued, Molly,' Alison warned her. 'Or this shark will cheat you.'

It was a lovely spring day and Molly had the windows open out on to her balcony. The gulls wheeled, squawking, along the cliff top, only feet from them.

'What a magnificent view,' Ralph said, wandering out on to the balcony. 'I can just make out the coastline of Wales but you can't see the bay at all.'

'The cliff makes an odd turn just here. The only inhabited place with a good view of the bay is the Crows Nest. You can see it clearly from the cliff path, of course.'

'What cliff path?'

'It runs from here to the Crow.'

'It's awful,' Alison said. 'It's about two feet wide and a sheer drop over the side.'

'Don't be silly, Alison,' Molly said. 'It's a good eight feet wide. I take Castlemaine for a walk there every night.'

'That's the trouble with dogs,' Ralph said gloomily. 'Always wanting walkies. My mother-in-law, Baroness Turnbull, keeps dozens of them and she expects me to take them out tramping through the mud when we go to visit.'

'Never mind, Ralph. I don't suppose you'll get invited any more,' Alison said, earning a sour look for her pains.

'I enjoy it,' Molly said. 'We never see a soul. It's so dark and peaceful, I feel as if I'm in another world. Just the stars and the lights from the bay. Everyone around here is in bed by eleven, you know. I can pretend I'm the only human being left on the planet.'

'Aren't you worried?' Alison asked. 'What about this murderer on the loose?'

'Ah now, Alison, I want to know all about that. I don't want to sound ghoulish but you must have all the details.'

'Just what everyone else knows,' Alison said, remembering what Nick had said about 'pillow talk'. Molly looked disappointed.

'It's not that I'm a gossip,' she lied. Ralph and Alison both perish-the-thoughted briskly. Molly vied with Aunt Avis for the title of Chief Information Disseminator for the valley. 'But the annoying thing about Nick Trevellyan is he's so conscientious. Are you sure he hasn't told you any interesting details, Alison?'

'I need a drink,' Ralph said, after they had left Molly. 'Where shall we go?'

'What about the Crows Nest. That's nearest.'

'Nick's uncle's pub?'

'That's a point. Uncle Lynton will think I'm up to no good, drinking with strange men.'

'He's not your uncle. It's none of his business.'

'I shall just have to explain, that's all.'

'Might as well walk there, I suppose. So long as we don't fall over the edge.'

They took the narrow cliff path up towards the Crow. After about two hundred yards they rounded the corner and saw the Hop Bay sparkling beneath them in the spring sunshine.

'Quite impressive,' Ralph admitted.

'We're nearly there. Just round this second corner.' Alison examined her watch. 'Just the right time for a pre-lunch drinkie.' She pushed open the door of the bar which was, at first glance, deserted. Then Lynton popped up from behind the counter.

'Alison! How nice to see you.' He looked narrowly at Ralph.

'Hello, Lynton,' Alison said. 'This is Ralph Squires. He's an old friend of mine, staying with us for a few days. Poor Nick is terribly busy with the Carstairs murder.' Lynton merely nodded.

'Two large G and Ts,' was all Ralph said.

'Old college friend,' Alison babbled. 'Someone to keep me company while poor Nick is so busy.' Ralph looked at her as if she'd taken leave of her senses. She half expected Lynton to wag his finger and say, "The lady doth protest too much, methinks," but he obviously didn't know that one.

'Yes, I heard about that, poor kid,' he said instead. 'Hello, Ralph. Surely you and Nick brought him in once before, Alison.'

'Oh yes, that's right. Clever of you to remember.'

'I've got a good memory for faces,' Lynton said as he passed their drinks over the counter. 'Useful in this line. You're actually staying at Hope Cottage, are you, Ralph?'

'Sure thing,' Ralph said. 'Very comfortable billet. Charming company too.' He raised his glass to Alison.

'Yes,' Lynton said. 'Quite so. Charming.'

Lynton had the dark curls and the almost Latin complexion which all the Trevellyans shared. Alison wondered why she had never noticed that Ben Lawson too had this distinctive colouring, in sharp contrast to the wispy pallor of Alan and Sam. It was a look which suited men best; the hair a little too indisciplined, the features too strong to flatter a woman. Alison hoped that her daughters would not look like Margaret or Avis.

'Good morning!' Ralph said appreciatively and Alison looked round and smiled at the more delicate features of Lorna Trevellyan, a much better advertisement for the family DNA. Ralph switched the charm up to maximum, bought Lorna a drink and launched into his best chat-up routine. Lorna, whose gipsy loveliness housed a practical—even suburban—soul, had her sights firmly fixed on Edward Savage's consumptive beauty, not to mention his comfortable income and the status which the position of doctor's wife conferred in a small town. But she parried Ralph's efforts with good-natured amusement while her sharp eyes did not overlook the white mark on his left hand where his wedding ring had so recently been.

The dark shadows which Nick had noticed round Dr Savage's eyes were not the result of overwork or the burden of ministering to the sick, as he had conjectured, but caused by the late nights the doctor spent pursuing Lorna after closing time; compounded by acute sexual frustration resulting from protestations of virtue from the young woman which would have astonished quite a few men in the valley.

Lorna was flirting obligingly with Ralph to keep her hand in. Alison was left to talk to Lynton who was looking at her thoughtfully.

'You look a lot like Hannah in that get up,' he said. Alison had donned her country-gentlewoman mantle for Ralph's benefit and was wearing twin-set, tweeds and lavender water.

'What?'

'Hannah. My sister-in-law. Nick's mother. She was a redhead, you know.'

'No, I didn't know.' The only photograph Alison had seen of Hannah Trevellyan showed her white-haired and elderly.

'Oh, yes,' Lynton said. 'Fine head of ginger hair she had as a girl. I expect that's what attracted Nick to you in the first place.'

'God preserve us from amateur psychiatrists.' Ralph, whose suggestion that Lorna might care to meet him later had been met with a good-natured but firm rebuff, interrupted the conversation waspishly.

'I think it's nice enough to go out into the garden,' Alison said.

'Oh, definitely,' Ralph said.

'Kit's out there,' Lynton said. 'Making holes in his fishing nets.'

'You mean mending them, Lynton,' Alison explained kindly.

'No, I don't. Mending them is what he does when any tourists are watching. He pretends to be a fisherman, mending his nets, and gets them to take a trip round the bay in our boat. But as he never does any fishing, he has to make the holes ready. He's hoping for some tourists soon—now that we're past Easter.'

'Very enterprising,' Alison said after a short pause.

'It's about all he's fit for,' Lynton called after them as they went out through the rear door.

'It's not bad here,' Ralph decided, looking round the clifftop garden.

'No. We come here quite often when the weather's nice.'

'We, we, we,' Ralph said crossly. 'You sound like a suburban housewife.' Alison, who always found herself reverting to adolescence in Ralph's company, stuck her tongue out at him. 'You've never carried on like this before. Even all those years you lived with Gareth Dalston.'

'It was only two years.'

'You sure had the hots for Gareth, all right.'

'At first, maybe. By the time he shoved off back to Johannesburg I couldn't have cared less.'

Ralph looked sceptical. 'Didn't look that way from where I was standing.'

Alison leant on the white wooden fence which prevented drunken patrons from tumbling headlong into the bay and looked down over the waves. She did not speak for a moment, then her head still turned carefully away, she said: 'Gareth was unfaithful to me all the time. Once, I remember, we went to a party in Hampstead and he actually went off with another woman. He didn't come home for two days. Then he just behaved as if nothing had happened. I was glad to see the back of him. Nobody treats me like that, Ralph.' She turned to face him at last. 'No one's ever going to get the chance to treat me like that again.' Ralph patted her shoulder with a surge of something like real affection.

'Hi,' said Kit Trevellyan, who had crept up on them unawares. Ralph jumped. Nick's young cousin was disconcertingly like him—only shorter and stockier and more dishevelled like an earlier, and not wholly successful, draft.

'If it isn't honorary-cousin Alison,' he said, 'with a strange man.' He gave her a not-very cousinly kiss on the cheek which she didn't remember ever inviting him to do and eyed Ralph with amusement. 'He's got a guilty conscience. Did you see the way he jumped just then?'

'If you will creep up on people like that, Kit. I've just been hearing about your net-mending exploits.'

'Hmm, a tourist and his money are soon parted. Beats helping Lorna behind the bar anyway.'

'Ever thought of getting a proper job?' Alison asked, in her best impersonation of the Prime Minister.

Kit obviously recognised it because he grinned and said: 'I'm part of the new enterprise culture, Alison. But you can take me on in your computer firm if you like.'

'I don't need any nets mended, thanks. Where's this boat of yours? I didn't know you had one.'

'Just down in the harbour, with the fishing smacks. If you stand very close to the edge of the cliff and lean over, you can see it. No? Well you'll have to take the cliff railway down to the beach then.'

'I'm not going anywhere until I've had another drink,' Ralph said. 'I'll just pop inside and get us some refills.'

'Good idea,' Kit said. 'Mine's a pint, Ralph.'

'Oh, all right,' Ralph said.

FOURTEEN

BILL DROPPED NICK at Hope Cottage at four o'clock on their way back from Great Hopford and an abortive interview with the gossipy old lady who ran the sub post office. She knew of no elderly men with greyhounds in the village. 'And who would know him if not me?' she'd said reasonably. Nick was growing disheartened.

'I'll just get a shower and change and then I'll see you back at base,' he said, as he closed the passenger door. Alison's Jaguar and Ralph's red Porsche, with its distinctive numberplate—RS 666, huddled close as new lovers in the courtyard.

Nick went into the house and called out, but of Alison and Ralph there was neither sight nor sound. He went up to his and Alison's bedroom and fetched some clean towels from the dressing room. The door out on to the balcony was open and, on impulse, he walked out for a moment to enjoy the spring sunshine.

Looking down across the lawn he saw Alison and Ralph sitting in the summerhouse. He could not see them very clearly since the willow branches had drooped down over the panes of glass. He was about to call out to them when he saw, to his horror, that Ralph and Alison were kissing. Ralph had his arms locked rightly around Alison and was running his fingers through her glorious hair.

Shattered, Nick turned away and went in a daze into the bathroom. In a moment he was under the shower.

He could not have said if it ran hot or cold—or if the water streaming down his face came from the shower head, or from his own eyes.

If he had watched a few seconds longer, he would have seen Ralph start back angrily as a well aimed kick made contact with his left shin.

'Christ, Alison!' he snapped, hopping on one leg. 'That hurt.'

'Don't you ever try to do that again.'

'That was bloody uncalled-for!'

'I warn you, Ralph, next time it won't be your shin. I'll make your eyes water.'

'Provincial,' he said in disgust. 'I knew living in this God-forsaken hole would turn you bloody provincial.'

'If being faithful to Nick—and not letting myself be groped by any man who happens to feel like it—is provincial, then I'll be bloody provincial and glad of it.'

They glared at each other in fury for a full half minute then, suddenly, they both burst out laughing.

'No hard feelings?' Ralph said, sitting down again and rubbing his leg. 'After all you can't blame a bloke for trying.'

'No hard feelings, Ralph. But I meant what I said. Next time it will be straight in the balls. Don't say you weren't warned. Come on. It's tea time.'

They walked back across the lawn, laughing and chattering, the best of friends again. Nick joined them on the terrace fifteen minutes later, feeling refreshed from his shower but otherwise in a state approaching despair.

'Nick!' Alison said happily. 'You don't usually get home this early. Especially when you're working on a case.' She turned her face up to be kissed. Nick dropped a very small peck on her forehead.

'No. I can't stay. I just came home to change.'

'You've got time for some tea, surely.'

'No. I've got to get back now. Bye. Have a nice evening.'

He drove back to the police station rather fast. He was furious with himself for not saying anything. Still there would be time enough to have it out later. Or did he want to have it out? Would he rather not know?

At ten o'clock, after hours of bouncing ideas back and forth with Bill, Nick was still no nearer a clear picture of the murder scene than he had been on Monday night. And they were not finished yet. He wondered if he should ring Alison and say he would sleep at his flat that night.

'I'm damned if I will,' he said aloud.

'What's that, sir?' Bill said.

'Nothing. Just thinking aloud.'

Two and a half hours later Nick pushed all the papers away into his desk, locked it and said: 'Let's push off home now, Bill. See you back here in the morning.' He was damned if he was going to leave the field clear for slimy Ralph Squires without so much as a fight.

When he got to Hope Cottage the house was in darkness. Alison was fast asleep. Normally Nick was very quiet when he came home late but tonight he deliberately made quite a lot of noise as he undressed and washed, hoping that she would wake up. Then he'd have it out with her. He even switched on the light on his bedside table but Alison slept soundly through it all—her breathing deep and regular, the suspicion of a snore. She had not been in bed long as she was still pink and damp from her bath. Had she spent the evening making love with Ralph? Was that why she was now sleeping so soundly, why she had taken care to have a bath? He examined her peaceful face, pale against the mane of red on the lacy pillow. He leant over and kissed her parted lips gently. She did not stir. She smelt of brandy and talcum powder.

'Alison,' he whispered into her unreceptive ear, 'I love you so much. I can't live without you.'

He set his alarm for seven-thirty and switched off the light. He blanked out his troubled mind, as he had trained himself to do over the years, and fell quickly into a restless sleep.

HE WAS DEEPLY ASLEEP when the alarm went off. He groaned and reached out to turn it off. Alison also groaned, turned over, said 'What the hell time is it?' and went back to sleep without waiting for an answer. Nick's head was heavy. He sat on the edge of the bed for a moment trying to wake up. Alison turned over again and put an arm round his waist amorously. He disentangled himself. She put her arm round him again and stroked his thigh. He stood up.

'Don't get up yet, Nick,' she said, properly awake at last. 'It's only half-past seven. Come back to bed for a while.'

Nick went into the dressing room and began to pull his clothes on. 'I'm not in the mood,' he called back into the bedroom.

'I can soon remedy that.' Alison sat up, the bed-clothes falling away so she was naked to the waist. Nick stared at her dry-mouthed; half of him looking for treacherous bites or scratches; the other half not wanting to look.

'Is something wrong?' she said, puzzled. He didn't reply. 'I can't do anything about it if you don't tell me what it is. Is it something I've done to upset you? Or is something new on the Frisco case?'

He stood in the dressing-room doorway and looked at her silently for a moment. Finally, he said, 'I saw you kissing Ralph in the garden yesterday.'

'Oh no you didn't.'

'Alison! I saw you.'

'You saw Ralph kissing me.' She jumped out of bed and ran over to him. He was fully dressed now. She was naked. She flung her arms round his neck and tried to kiss him but he turned his head away.

'Oh, I see,' he said coldly, 'a very fine distinction.'

'It's a big distinction. How long were you watching?'

'I turned away at once. I didn't think you'd want an audience.'

'In that case,' she said gently, 'you didn't see me kick him on the shin.'

'Oh?' Nick said sceptically.

'He just grabbed hold of me. Took me quite by surprise. I kicked him to make him let go. You must have happened to see us at exactly the wrong moment. I was furious with him.'

'You didn't look very furious when I saw you on the terrace just a few minutes later,' he pointed out.

'We made it up,' she said with a shrug. 'I don't hold it against him. It would be idiotic to make a fuss about a stupid little thing like that,' she said meaningfully.

'Get back to bed, Alison, you're shivering.'

'I'll go back to bed when you say you believe me.'

'Of course I believe you.' He put his arms round her and nuzzled her hair, overwhelmed with relief.

'Why didn't you *say* anything?' she said, wanting to shake him.

'I didn't have a chance. You were asleep when I got in last night.'

'But you were going to creep off this morning without a word, weren't you.'

'Probably,' he mumbled.

'If I hadn't tackled you about it, you would have been brooding over it and not saying anything for God knows how long, and I might never had the chance to explain. You'd have been making yourself unhappy and making poor Bill's life a misery too, most likely.'

'I'm sorry for doubting you.' He kissed her. 'Please go back to bed.'

'You ought to be careful, Nick. Remember what happened to that Othello bloke when he got a bee in his bonnet that his wife was putting it about.'

Nick laughed at this literary synopsis. 'I shall bear it in mind, if ever I have a wife.'

'I don't understand you, Nick. If I'd seen you kissing another woman I'd have been straight down there demanding an explanation. I'd have boxed your ears and kicked her halfway round the garden.'

'Yes, I know you would,' he said, with a smile. 'Call it a difference of temperament.'

'It's so much better not to bottle things up, Nick.'

'I can't change the way I am, my angel.'

She hopped back between the sheets and pulled the quilt up around her shoulders. 'Ralph tries it on with every woman he meets. He was chatting up Lorna yesterday lunchtime. He didn't get very far.'

'Good,' Nick said half seriously. 'Because if he comes sniffing round any of my womenfolk again, I shall thump him.'

'Cor! Scratch a new man and what do you find? Seriously, Nick, I'll tell Ralph to go today, if he's upsetting you.'

'There's no need for that. Well…you might just give him a hint, I suppose.'

WHEN NICK GOT HOME that evening there was no sign of Ralph's Porsche. He found Alison in the sitting room. She was stretched out on the window seat, her back against the shutter, reading *A Taste for Death*.

'Dare I hope that Repulsive Ralph has gone?' he asked, leaning over to kiss her.

'He's gone all right. All the way to Hopcliff to look at a Victorian linen chest.' Nick flopped down in the black leather armchair and mimed despair.

'I dropped him a very large hint,' Alison said. 'but he's got a hide like a rhino. It suits him very well to have free board and lodging here. I don't think we'll get rid of him until he's bought up all the bargains in the Hop Valley.'

'Bargains? You mean until he's swindled all the widows and orphans out of their good pieces?'

'People aren't that soft any more, Nick. They all watch *Antiques Roadshow*. When a man with a posh voice and a posh car and a smart suit tells them he'll take their grandmother's toilette table off their hands, they immediately take it off to be valued.'

'Fish and visitors stink after three days,' Nick said.

Alison giggled. 'I don't want to waste time talking about Ralph. He said he'd get something to eat out but I suspect he's going to the Crow to have another try at Lorna. He doesn't like being turned down—it hurts his vanity. So that just leaves you and me. Want to go out?'

'Can we just have an omelette or something and stay in and have an early night?'

'Of course. Mushroom soufflé omelette and green salad suit you?'

'That sounds wonderful. Thank you.'

'And I'll fetch something decent up from the cellar.'

Ralph got back just after eleven—pubs in the Valley closed at ten-thirty on Sunday. Nick was in the kitchen in his dressing gown, getting a glass of water for Alison. Ralph peered round the door. He smelt strongly of drink.

'Having an early night?' he leered. 'The little love-birds?' Nick took a large sip of water and considered throwing the rest in Ralph's grinning face. Pity it wasn't sulphuric acid to erase the smile permanently.

'How's the shin, Ralph?' he asked. Ralph stopped leering.

'She said she wouldn't tell you. Couldn't resist making you jealous, I suppose. How like the gentler sex.'

'She didn't tell me,' Nick replied, 'but next time you're doing anything you shouldn't make sure no one is watching you. Excuse me.' He walked out of the kitchen.

'Who says I shouldn't?' Ralph called after him. 'She's not your property, you know.' Nick ignored him and went back upstairs.

'He stinks of drink,' he complained to Alison. 'If I'd seen him get out of his car I'd have had him for drunk driving.'

'Honestly, Nick. You're not on traffic duty. I've never seen anyone drink as much as Ralph and be so little affected by it.'

'Tell that to the magistrates.'

'You're becoming obsessed by him. Forget about him. Aren't you coming back to bed?' She sat up, spreading her arms wide in invitation.

'Yes,' Nick said eagerly, untying his dressing gown. The phone began to ring. Alison collapsed back against the pillows with a groan.

'Shit! It's bound to be for you. Don't answer it.'

Nick refastened his dressing gown and picked up the receiver. 'Hope Cottage, Nick Trevellyan speaking... Oh, hello, Bill.'

Alison gave a low moan. She hissed, 'Surely it can't be that urgent. Tell him to sod off.' Nick motioned her to be quiet, he was listening intently.

'When did this happen? Where is she now? OK, I'll meet you up there in about half an hour.' He hung up. 'I'm sorry, Alison.'

'I suppose I can hold out.' She pressed her hand to her brow theatrically.

'Molly Armitage was attacked this evening while walking her dog on the cliff near her house. She's not dead,' he added hastily, seeing her horrified face, 'but she's in the hospital, in intensive care. The assailant tried to strangle her.' He went into the dressing room and began to dress hurriedly. Alison followed him and started to pull on a pair of jeans.

'What do you think you're doing?' Nick asked, as if he didn't know.

'Coming with you of course. She's my godmother.'

Nick knew better than to argue. 'All right, I'll drop you at the hospital.'

'I wasn't expecting this,' he said, as he made a right turn out of Hope Cottage five minutes later and headed for Hopbridge. 'I thought Frisco was a one off. A killing with a motive. This is a poser.'

He dropped Alison at the hospital and headed off to Hopcliff to meet Bill as arranged.

BILL WAS THERE BEFORE HIM and had got everything organised. Under brilliant arc lights, the Scene of Crime team and photographers were busy on the cliff path.

'She was out walking her dog,' Bill said. 'Apparently she does it every night at about half-past ten or eleven, usually along the cliff path. It's a dark, deserted sort of place at night. There's not many would fancy it.'

'She's lived here for quite a few years, in that house. She must have known every inch of the path. What time do we reckon the attack took place?'

'As near eleven as makes no difference. The dog gave the alarm; ran up to that bungalow on the other side of the ridge; woke them up with its barking—or yapping, more like. There's no reason to suppose that the dog hung about for half an hour before raising the alarm. It's a Mr and Mrs Gloucester. They found Lady Armitage unconscious. When the strangler let go of her she fell and hit her head on an overhanging rock. That seems to be the worst of the injury, ironically enough. They're waiting for you to see them now.'

'Did they see anyone?'

'No one passed them on the path, that's for sure. They were tucked up in bed when they heard the dog going berserk. And there was hardly any moon tonight. Is it a serial killer, Mr Trevellyan? Miss Carstairs, now Lady Armitage?'

'Unlikely I'd say,' Nick said, trying to reassure himself as much as Bill. 'Two such different women in age and class. They tend to stick to a type.' God help them if it was a serial murderer, he added to himself. How the hell did you catch someone with no motive? 'Did you manage to get hold of Sir Anton?'

Bill nodded. 'He was at a committee meeting in town. He went straight to the hospital.'

'We'll have to check up on him. I'll drop in there on my way back. Alison's there.'

'Why did the killer leave the job unfinished, sir?'

'Who knows. Lady Armitage is over sixty and she's a small woman. He may have thought she was dead when she wasn't. Or the dog may have scared him off with its barking. Or someone else may have disturbed him. If so, let's hope they come forward. Or perhaps he didn't intend to kill her but just to scare her or rob her.'

'People don't take valuables when they walk the dog.'

'She would have had her house keys, though. Perhaps someone knew Sir Anton was out and wanted to burgle the house. Were her keys still on her?'

'Yes, but I'll leave a constable there until Sir Anton gets back.'

Nick spoke to the Gloucesters—an elderly couple, enjoying their brief notoriety. They were not the most reliable of witnesses, willing to agree that they had seen a tall man with a peg leg and a parrot on his shoulder leaving the scene of crime if Nick had suggested that they might have. He gave up and decided to leave it to the Scene of Crime team for the night. There was always a temptation to hang around getting in their way; Nick found it easy enough to resist tonight. He and Bill walked slowly back to their cars.

'What about the dog?' Bill asked.

'I'll take her home with me for the night.' A young PC brought the spaniel over. Nick picked her up and she began to lick his face stickily. There was something to be said for toy spaniels, Nick thought, you could use their ears to polish your shoes. Still, with a bit of prompting she might bite Ralph.

'What's the shortest time it would take to drive from here to Hope Cottage on a quiet night?' he asked suddenly.

Bill looked at him in surprise. 'I don't see how it could take less than fifteen minutes, what with having to go through Hopbridge. Why?'

'Oh nothing. Just wishful thinking.'

Alison was right. He was becoming obsessed. Nick found Alison and Anton in Molly's hospital room. Anton clasped his hand warmly.

'Thank goodness you're in charge, Nick. Couldn't be in better hands.'

'How is she?' Nick asked.

'Still unconscious but they gave her a brain scan and said there's no real damage. Just a bit of concussion. Hard head, my Molly.'

'They didn't want to let us stay with her,' Alison said. 'I had to be pretty firm with them.'

'That's my girl,' Anton said. 'You take young Alison home, Inspector. She can't do any good here. I'll stay the night. You make her get some rest and come back tomorrow, eh?' He patted her fondly on the bottom. 'Off you go, Alison.'

She trotted obediently out of the hospital room with Nick. In the corridor, he said, 'You wait for me in the car, it's parked round the side by casualty. I won't be a minute.' He gave her the keys. 'Castlemaine's in the back seat. Don't let her out.'

He went back to the private room and poked his head round the door. 'I should like to talk to you in the morning, Sir Anton.'

'Yes, of course. I shall be here until Molly comes round. Any time, my dear boy. You come and find me here when you want me and we'll nip round to the station and get it all down in writing.'

Nick thanked him, relieved that Anton was making it so easy for him. He drove himself and Alison home to bed.

FIFTEEN

'YOU'RE DISGUSTING, Nick Trevellyan!'

Nature had not economised on Alison's vocal cords and Castlemaine, already bewildered by her sudden change of abode, began to bark in distress at the ill-temper she sensed in her new family. Nick had to raise his voice to drown them out. The kitchen at Hope Cottage was as quiet as Kilburn High Road at chucking-out time on St. Patrick's Night.

'For God's sake, Alison! It's perfectly normal. I have to question Sir Anton to eliminate him from my enquiries.'

'Everyone knows they're devoted to each other. Isn't it bad enough for him to have Molly lying unconscious in hospital without some great clod of a policeman asking him to account for his movements? Harassing him.'

'I am not harassing him! All I want to know is where he was last night at eleven o'clock. I can't discount anything at this stage. This may be another attempt by the Frisco murderer or it may, just possibly, be that Sir Anton decided to get rid of his wife and do a copycat killing to fool everyone.'

'Oh yes,' Alison said sarcastically. 'Or perhaps he killed Frisco to provide a smokescreen for when he killed Molly.'

'Well, perhaps he did!'

'Pig!'

'Can't you come up with a more original insult?'
Nick stared at her, more in sorrow than in anger. When
she was in this sort of temper, there was no way to get
through to her. 'It's just the way things are,' he said
wearily. 'When a man or woman gets killed—attacked—the first person you question is the husband or
wife. Then the parents or children, brothers, sisters—'

'Cousins?'

'. . . Yes! I can't be held responsible for human nature, Alison. Surely you can understand.'

'No, I can't. I haven't got your foul policeman's
mind, thank God!'

Ralph appeared, grinning, in the doorway. 'Lover's
tiff?' he drawled. 'Shouting too loud to hear the
phone? It's for you, Nick.'

Nick spoke shortly into the telephone. Then he put
on his coat and went out of the front door.

'Lady Armitage has recovered consciousness,' he
called over his shoulder. 'So I'm off to harass her now,
OK?'

ALISON WENT TO SEE MOLLY that afternoon. She was
propped up against the pillows looking rather white.
Anton was still there and greeted Alison happily.

'Just what Molly needs: her favourite goddaughter
come to cheer her up.'

Alison planted a kiss on Molly's cheek and sat down.
Anton patted her knee in what he imagined was an
avuncular manner.

'Had a long talk with your young man this morning,' he said. 'He was so polite and charming. Seemed
almost to be apologising for troubling me. I understood what he was after, of course. Stands to reason,

if someone gets done in, the one with the motive is the long-suffering spouse, eh, Molly?'

'If it had been you who was attacked, Anton, he could have had the handcuffs on me straight away.'

'But didn't you mind?' Alison said, in bewilderment. 'When he kept questioning me, after Aidan was killed, sometimes I had to clench my fists to stop myself from hitting him.'

'Nonsense. He's just doing his job. I tell you he was perfectly charming.'

'He was very kind to me this afternoon too,' Molly said. 'I've never told you how much I like him, have I, Alison? When you stare death in the face you realise all the things you've left unsaid. You know how much I love you, dear. He's just the man for you: gentle and loving; but strong enough to stand up to you too and not let you bully him—unless I'm very much mistaken.'

'I thought you didn't approve,' Alison said, in surprise. 'You've hardly mentioned him since he moved in with me.'

'I wasn't sure at first, I admit it. I thought maybe you had a bad attack of the gratitudes after he saved your life, but then, seeing you both together so often, seeing you grow daily calmer and happier, I realised it wasn't that at all, and then I was too...embarrassed.'

'That's not like you.'

'Not about the living together "in sin", I don't give a single hoot about that. Oh, I know it still raises a few eyebrows in this sleepy backwater—despite *Eastenders*. But the eyebrows of the Hop Valley can stay in a permanent state of erection for all I care.'

Alison smiled at the image. 'What then?'

'You were always such a private girl. Even as a small child, you didn't like anyone to see what you really felt. When you fell over and grazed your knee you would sit there with your lip trembling, willing yourself not to cry.'

'Most people would say that I make my feelings felt only too strongly,' Alison said, stamping on this mawkishness before Molly sent Anton home for the baby photos.

'On trivial matters perhaps,' Molly went on, undeflected. 'Well, I love you dearly and I could see how much you felt about him and I thought, you being the sort of girl—sorry, woman—you are, that you'd prefer not to talk about it. Well, the ice is broken now and we shall speak of it again. But it's what I mean about the things left unsaid. At least your generation is more outspoken, in general, than ours. If there's one piece of advice I can give my goddaughter before I die—which I now realise could be at any time—it is not to let things slide through lack of communication, or through pride.'

BILL DROVE HIMSELF and Nick back up to Hopcliff that night to interview anyone who might have been leaving the Crow's Nest the previous night at about eleven. The moon had waned almost completely and it was dark inside the car. Nick felt in need of a confidant.

'Why do couples who love each other waste precious time quarrelling?' he asked. Bill glanced round at his boss in surprise, decided the question was rhetorical and drove on in silence. 'What do you think, Bill?' Nick persisted.

Not rhetorical after all. Bill pondered; he had considerably more respect than liking for Alison. His instinct was to say that she was an arrogant, bad-tempered, quarrelsome sort of woman so what could you expect?

'Life's a compromise at best, isn't it? There's always things to quarrel about,' he said finally.

'Do you and Susie quarrel?'

'Yeah, of course.'

'What about? Sorry. Look, tell me to mind my own business if you like.'

'It's OK. I reckon over the years we've quarrelled mostly about money and the children.'

'Oh?'

'It's what most couples row about. Money: 'cause there isn't usually quite enough and one woman's necessity is another man's extravagance. The kids: well, Susie always said I was too soft with the girls and I thought she was too hard on them. That was when they were little. Now Sarah's old enough to go out with boys the boot seems to be on the other foot. Susie lets her stay out 'til all hours while I want to give the boys the third degree before I let them so much as carry her books home from school.'

Nick sighed. 'Alison and I haven't any children and we haven't any money worries either.'

'Miss Hope likes to get her own way and she's used to ploughing her own furrow, and so are you. It's early days yet for you and her. It takes a little while to learn to give and take.' Bill began to wonder if there was any limit to the number of clichés you could string together at random. But that was the thing about clichés—they were usually true. He also realised that what his boss wanted was a sympathetic ear and not a serious answer to unanswerable questions.

'Did Susie ever worry about your job?' Nick asked. 'I don't mean the danger you might be in personally or the bloody awful hours but the implications of it. Interrogating people, even bullying them sometimes. People you may know and like.'

'Oh, I see. The answer is yes and she never really has got used to it. She's got more philosophical though, over the years. She realises now it's them or us. When I joined the force they still hadn't abolished hanging. Think about that, charging someone knowing they're going to the gallows, then having to go home and kiss the children goodnight and read them a bedtime story.'

'Did that every happen to you?'

'No, thank God. I was still an innocent uniformed constable when they did away with it, telling people the time and standing on the touchline at football matches. Things were different in those days.'

They were both silent for a few minutes then Nick tried again.

'Do you think it's possible to love someone too much?'

Although the lights of Hopcliff were now up ahead it was still very dark in the car. Bill wondered if his boss would have spoken to him like this in the daylight and whether he would regret it later. After a long pause he said, 'It's not something I know much about.'

'I didn't mean to embarrass you.'

'You're not embarrassing me, Nick. It's just I've been married twenty years and there are so many other things to worry about by then: children and pensions and your old parents and so on. You don't give it much thought any more. But to answer your question as best

I can, I don't think normal people like you and Miss Hope can love each other too much. It's only with the inadequates where it can turn sour. Here we are at the Crow.'

He pulled the car to a halt and looked at his boss under the car park lights. 'Miss Hope is a girl in a million.' That wasn't exactly a lie, he told himself, there certainly weren't many about like her.

'Yes, she is,' Nick said, taking the statement at face value. 'That's why I couldn't bear to lose her.'

'Sir, I don't know Miss Hope that well, of course, despite the business with her cousin, but if you're asking my advice—well, you must stand up to her. She's a strong woman and she admires strength in other people. No offence.'

'None taken. Thanks, Bill.'

'Her tempers don't last very long, anyway.'

'That's true,' Nick said more cheerfully. Alison's anger was as fleeting and as unpredictable as an April shower. 'Let's go and have a word with Uncle Lynton.'

'That reminds me,' Bill said as they walked across the car park, 'it's our twentieth anniversary soon. Susie met Mrs Lorryson-Monday in the chemist's the other day.' Nick had no difficulty in recognising the usual Hopbridge corruption of Jean-Luc's outlandish surname. 'And now she keeps going on at me about taking her to Hopwood Manor.'

'You'll be sure of a good meal there.'

'Yeah, how many arms and legs will it cost me, though? That's what I'd like to know.'

'Oh, it's not that bad. You can get away with a few fingers and toes if you stick to the daily specials. Let me know when you're going and I'll get Meg to make sure you have a really good time.'

'She's a nice lady, Mrs Lorryson-Monday.' Bill liked everybody except criminals and Alan Lawson and Paul Penruan...and Alison. 'Trudi, my youngest, she's very keen on cookery and Mrs Lorryson was really nice to her. Said she could come and see a real restaurant kitchen in action if she wanted.'

'Meg's good with children.'

'Pity she hasn't got any of her own.'

'She and Jean-Luc spent every last penny on the Manor when they came back from France and then they did most of the renovation themselves. I suppose they had neither the time nor the money. I don't know that they're much bothered. Meg's never said anything about it. I imagine they're one of those couples who're perfectly happy—just the two of them.'

Bill began to whistle something which Nick recognised—just—as 'If you're going to San Francisco' and he realised that Bill's happy memories of that era were of his courtship and honeymoon with Susie and not any of the wilder theories of Nick's over-fertile imagination.

They went into the public bar where Lynton was usually to be found and where most of the regulars congregated. Lynton was there, polishing glasses vigorously.

'Hello, young Nick,' he said. 'Long time no see. What're you having?'

'Nothing thanks, Lynton. It's not a social call.' Nick hesitated for the moment, examining his uncle's familiar features for traces of Ben Lawson, then recollected himself and blushed. 'What have you done to your hand?' he asked hastily.

'Beer glass came apart while I was washing up. Great jagged bit went straight into my palm.'

'I hope you've had it seen to.'

'Naw,' Lynton said, scornfully. 'Lorna bandaged it up for me. It'll heal up in no time.'

'You must have heard what happened to Lady Armitage last night.'

'Yes, indeed, nasty business. She's such a nice little old lady.' Lynton hesitated and Nick smiled. People who started off saying that Molly Armitage was a nice little old lady usually thought better of it on reflection. 'They say she was strangled,' Lynton continued, letting the statement stand for the moment. 'Is it to do with that other death in your village?'

'I don't know yet. I want to talk to a few of your regulars who were in here just before eleven last night. I'm hoping someone saw something on the way home.'

'I'll do what I can. Actually Lorna was behind the bar most of last night. She's out the back. Go and have a word with her.' Lynton lifted the bar flap and they passed through a bead curtain into the back kitchen where Lorna was eating her supper with half an eye on the television.

'Nick! I haven't seen you for ages.' She jumped up, flung her arms round his neck and kissed him soundly.

'Hey,' he said, extricating himself. 'You're very pleased with yourself tonight, Lorna.'

She held out her left hand triumphantly for Nick to admire the large diamond on her ring finger.

'Four hundred quids' worth,' she said.

'Very nice,' Nick said. 'Who's the unfortunate man?'

'Edward Savage.'

'What? Doctor Savage?' Lorna nodded. 'Congratulations. How did you manage that, or shouldn't I ask?'

'Cynic,' she said good-naturedly.

'I wondered why he was looking so haggard when I saw him the other day. Now I know.'

'Laugh all you like, Nick. There'll be no more serving behind the bar for me when I'm the doctor's wife.'

'I expect you'll lie on the sofa all day having grapes peeled for you by the servants,' Nick said solemnly. 'When's it to be?'

'Soon as poss.'

'Don't give the poor chap time to come to his senses, eh?'

'You carry on like this and you won't get an invite.'

'I'll see if I can come up with any good impediments before the day.'

'I don't notice anyone wanting to marry you,' she said tartly.

'No.' Nick said. 'Nor do I. Well, this isn't a social call, Lorna. You were serving in the bar last night, so your dad tells me.'

'That's right. All evening.'

'Remember who was in?'

'There was half a dozen regulars; some yanks who were visiting our "biuful lil town", but they pushed off quite early after they'd been fleeced at shove-halfpenny. Sundays are always pretty quiet.'

'Can you make a list of the regulars and tell me who's here tonight and give me the addresses of the rest?'

'Yes, officer.'

'What time did you get rid of the last of them?'

'Why, we called time at half-past ten, Inspector,' Lorna said innocently, 'like we always do except Fridays and Saturdays.'

'Yes, dear. But what time did you actually close?'

'Well, the last ones were still here—just Dad's personal guests, you understand—when Edward and I got back at about one o'clock...'

'God! No wonder he's got bags under his eyes.'

'...but we actually closed the doors just on eleven.' She beamed at him. 'After Constable Protheroe had finished his third pint.'

'I didn't hear that.' Like most policemen, Nick suffered frequently from political deafness.

'Which way did Protheroe go when he left?' Bill put in.

'Um, off towards the town.'

'Not towards the cliff path?'

'No, because Edward and I were going that way and he called after us to be good and not to do anything he would do.'

'Hang on. Are you saying you and Savage were on the cliff path at eleven?'

'No.' Lorna giggled. 'We changed our minds and went for a drive in Edward's car instead. That was when he finally asked me.'

'Pity.'

'It's all right for you blokes. I'm not getting any younger, you know. I won't see,' she considered, weighing up vanity against plausibility, 'twenty-three again.'

'I meant it was a pity you didn't walk along the cliff path. You might have seen Lady Armitage's assailant, or your presence might even have prevented the attempt.'

'Sorry. You should have given me advance warning.'

'We'll be out in the bar talking to some of the regulars,' Nick said. 'Get the list done nice and quick, sweetie, and I'll buy you a decent wedding present.'

'You damn well will anyway,' Lorna said.

IT WAS PAST ELEVEN when Nick got home. There was no sign of Ralph's car and the house was in darkness. He went into the sitting room, sat down in the leather armchair and began to leaf through Alison's book. He heard her come in just a few minutes later. She poked her head round the door.

'Hello,' he said stiffly, 'you're late.'

She walked in and closed the door behind her. 'How big an apology do you want?' she demanded. 'Will abject do, or must I grovel at your feet?'

Nick shook his head, not as a negative but to check that his hearing was functioning correctly. He laid the book down on the side table.

'I bet Adam Dalgleish doesn't get criticised just for doing his job,' he said childishly. Alison replied that Adam Dalgleish was a fictional character. She perched on the arm of Nick's chair. He pulled her on to his lap.

'Not like you to apologise,' he said.

'I don't think I did in the end, did I?'

'No, I suppose not.'

'But I will, just this once. Sorry.' She bent her head and kissed him on the mouth. Then she removed his glasses and put them down on the book.

'Ah! Glasses-off kiss,' he said.

'Mmmm.'

'Have you been at the hospital all this time?' Nick asked, when he'd got his breath back.

'The hospital bouncers chucked us out at eight-thirty. Anton insisted on buying me dinner at the

Pheasant. He's very good company really. I felt an awful fool because he kept saying that my "Young Man" was terribly polite and charming.'

'Um, well. He is on the Police Authority. We think twice before beating a confession out of him.'

'He kept on about how lucky he was—that Molly wasn't lying dead—whereas most people would have been bemoaning their bad luck. Both the Armitages made me feel rather small today.'

'What did Lady Armitage tell you about the attack?'

'But you must have questioned her about it for ages. She has no idea who attacked her.'

'It was all very unsatisfactory. She gave me nothing at all. There has to be something: a sound, a smell, the reaction of her dog to the man, the feel of his clothing—wool, leather. She told me nothing. I'd like you to talk to her some more, Alison. She may know something in her subconscious which may suddenly come to the surface. Or, more seriously, she may have an inkling of who the attacker was.'

'But she would tell you at once!'

'No, not necessarily. She may be unsure and not want to point the finger, or it may be someone she knows and likes and she wants to tackle them herself.'

'Oh, Nick!'

'My foul policeman's mind, I'm afraid. Please listen carefully to what she says, Alison. If she does know who it was she will be in much worse danger.'

'You think he'll try again?'

'If it was a personal attack on Molly Armitage then he will have more reason than ever to silence her. If it was the Hop Valley Strangler he will probably turn his attention to a more unwary target.'

'Is there a Strangler?'

'Yesterday, I would have said not. I was sure Frisco was killed by someone who knew her, for a reason—however bizarre. Then this.'

'If someone wanted to get rid of Molly, surely it would have been more sensible just to push her over the cliff.'

'Agreed. Quicker and more certain. Which means either that this was the second in a series of attacks—in which case I shall have to stop questioning everyone who knew Frisco and start looking for a psychopath; or else someone wants it to look that way.

'And if it is a psychopath,' he went on slowly, 'we may not catch up with him until he kills again...or again.'

'Oh God, Nick!' Alison shivered.

'Bill's gone home to lock up his daughters. I suppose it's no good my trying to lock you up?'

'Not much good, no.'

Alison buried her head in his shoulder. Nick made soothing noises as his hands began to explore the warm folds of her body beneath her jersey.

LATER, as they lay waiting for sleep, their fingers gently interlaced in the middle of the bed, she said, 'We must learn to trust each other more, Nick.'

'Yes.'

'It hurt me that you thought I'd been messing about with Ralph. I thought you knew me better than that.'

'I'm so...unsure of you.' His fingers clutched at hers convulsively.

'You mean you really don't trust me?'

'I don't mean that exactly. I mean I don't know how you feel about me.'

'I think you do.'

'But you don't say it. You never tell me you love me. Once or twice at the beginning but not since.'

Alison sighed. 'And you, you say you love me all the time, but you won't always confide in me. Oh, I know you tell me about your work when you're supposed not to and I'm grateful for that because otherwise I would feel completely excluded from the most important thing in your life—'

'It's not the most important thing. Not any more.'

'—but sometimes I feel as if that's just a sop to keep me happy, make me think you trust me.'

'I was an old bachelor. I'm not used to sharing my feelings. Be patient with me.'

'I knew when I met you that you were sort of reserved, secretive almost, but I thought you'd opened out a bit since we've been together. Then something upsets you and you pull up the drawbridge and leave me on the other side of the moat. Half the time I can't tell what's going on inside your head.'

'I suppose I just can't believe my luck. That someone like you, who could have any man you wanted, should love me. If you do love me.' She did not reply. After a moment he went on, 'I keep thinking that one day another man will walk into your life, someone rich and important and dynamic, and you'll say "Ah yes, he's the one I've been waiting for."'

'That night you came here—after the end of the Aidan business—with your black eye, those were almost the very words I said to myself.' There was a pause then she said:

'I love you, Nick.'

'Thanks. Sorry to be so pathetically insecure.'

'It's not something I've ever been very good at saying. Some people say it all the time and don't mean it. When I first went to the States I was struck by the way people kept saying it to all their family and friends. It seemed so odd. I just couldn't get used to it. If you say it too often it begins to lose its magic power. The Hopes aren't great ones for talking about their feelings. We're an inhibited lot.'

'I've never found you inhibited. Rather the opposite.'

'Bed, you mean? That's just bodies, physical.'

'I hoped it was something rather more than that,' he said tenderly.

'You know what I mean. I never told you about my father, did I?'

'No.' Nick turned over on his side towards her. He could just see her shape in the darkness, lying on her back, her legs bent making a tent in the quilt. 'What about him?'

'He was over forty when he got married. My mother was thirty-five. He was a vicar and she was an archdeacon's daughter so everybody kept going on about how *suitable* it was, all his parishioners, the bishop, everyone. I never knew my grandfather but he was a bit of an old tyrant by all accounts, like the way he never spoke to my uncle again after he converted to Roman Catholicism. So when Dad told him that he was getting married at last, Grandfather was very pleased. He actually told Dad that marriages of convenience were usually the most successful. Poor Dad was too shy to tell him that he was passionately in love with my mother.' Alison laughed. Nick, who found the story rather sad, did not laugh.

'I hope he wasn't too shy to tell your mother the truth,' he said.

'He told me that story after the funeral. I came home from Cambridge for a few days to be with him. There was just the two of us. It was as if I had never really known him before. I never felt so close to him as I did at that moment.'

Nick smiled to himself; visualising the meek, middle-aged Hopes—familiar to him from photographs—bewildered by the big, bossy cuckoo which had hopped into their nest, just when they had reconciled themselves to childlessness. He gave his sleepy fancy full rein: seeing them all living two decades of mutual incomprehension, cushioned with love; the older Hopes wondering perhaps, from time to time, if they'd brought the wrong baby home from the hospital.

'Were you born in hospital?' he asked drowsily.

'No, at home,' Alison said in astonishment. 'What strange questions you ask.'

'Just wondered.' Nick had never felt so close to Alison as he did at that moment.

SIXTEEN

MOLLY ARMITAGE was allowed home the following day and Alison went over to Hopcliff to see her and return her dog. Ralph went with her.

'Might as well clinch the deal for the bureau. She can spend the money on a nice holiday to recuperate,' he said.

Molly pooh-poohed the idea. 'Where would I go?' she said scornfully. 'The seaside? This is the seaside. I shall sit here on my balcony and enjoy the view of the sea in spring. I may even get my sketch pad out.'

'I think you should consider it, Molly,' Alison said. 'At least until Nick has got the Hop Valley Strangler safely behind bars.'

'The what? Please don't talk like a tabloid newspaper, Alison.'

'While we all admire dear Nick's abilities,' drawled Ralph, 'he shows no sign of getting near locking anyone away at the moment. Except me, of course.' He giggled. 'He looks at me as if he'd like to put me in an *oubliette*.'

'Yes, well,' Molly said. 'More tea anyone?'

THE NEXT MORNING Bill drove himself and Nick up to Hopwood at the head of the valley to enquire, fruitlessly, about the old man on the moors. Nick hardly spoke at all on the drive back, his mind sorting through a rag bag in which all the rags came from different garments and would not make a decent pocket handkerchief between them. As Little Hopford came into view he said suddenly, 'Let's pull into Hope Cottage for a decent cup of coffee, then you might as well go home for a few hours. I shall be calling you out tonight, I'm afraid.'

Bill slowed the car down as they reached the corner. 'Are you sure Miss Hope won't mind?'

'Of course not.'

'Only...'

'What?'

'Well, I thought she'd killed her cousin, as you know. I wouldn't blame her if she held it against me.'

'She doesn't know. How could she?'

'You didn't tell her?'

'Certainly not. It's just your guilty conscience that's troubling you. No sign of Ralph's car, good.'

'Is it Miss Hope's friend who owns the red Porsche?'

'That's right.'

'Drives it at quite a speed, doesn't he?'

'Tell the traffic boys to keep a special look out for him, will you?'

At the sound of the car in the courtyard Alison appeared at the kitchen window and waved.

'She's still in her dressing gown,' Bill said nervously.

'She's been giving herself a holiday since she finished her latest game. Apart from making the vicar's life a misery, of course. Being lazy makes her sleepy. Come on.' Nick led the way through the conservatory into the kitchen.

'Any chance of some coffee?' he asked.

'I've just made a fresh pot. Do you want any breakfast?'

'Breakfast! It's nearly lunchtime, idle child.'

'Hello, Bill.'

'Good morning, Miss Hope.'

'I wish you wouldn't call me that. Why don't you call me Alison? Everyone does.'

'I'll try,' he said doubtfully. He sat down on a stool and took a cup of the strong coffee which Alison poured for him.

'Dot rang, yet again, to say she wasn't coming in to-day,' Alison told Nick. 'If she gives notice I shall hold you responsible.'

Nick laughed. 'Naturally!' He was leaning against the sink. She poured him a cup of coffee too and handed it to him. They stood very close together for a moment and his hand went up automatically to brush the hair away from her face and lingered lovingly on her cheek. They gazed into each other's eyes, quite oblivious of Bill's presence.

'I DIDN'T KNOW where to look really,' he told Susie after lunch, recalling the scene. 'Wondered if I ought just to make myself scarce. I felt like a peeping tom.'

'You're a right old misery,' Susie said. 'Remember what you said to me when you got home after Aidan Hope's funeral? "I give it six weeks, Suse," you said. That was nine months ago and they're still as crazy about each other as they were that day. So you can keep your Cassandra predictions to yourself.'

'"Crazy" about sums it up as far as he's concerned,' Bill said. 'Dunno so much about her, though.'

'It's just that she doesn't wear her heart on her sleeve. You only have to see the way she looks at him when she thinks nobody is watching.'

'I hope you're right.'

'I'm quite surprised they're not married already.'

'They would be if it was up to him.'

'Oh?'

'Don't repeat that to anyone, will you?'

'Of course not.'

'That's one of the things that worries me. I mean, if she really cared about him, she'd want to marry him, wouldn't she? I mean, women always want to get married. They don't give a bloke time to breathe as a rule before they're out choosing the curtains and carpets.'

'You sexist pig, you.'

'It's true,' Bill protested. 'Take me and you. We'd only been courting about three months and you were dropping hints so loud they could hear them in Plymouth—thought the *Luftwaffe* were up to their old tricks.'

'Are you looking for a thick ear?' Susie asked affectionately.

'Only...Mr Trevellyan. I...'

'Love him,' Susie prompted.

'Well, yeah. Like a kid brother, I mean,' he added hurriedly. 'He's always been so quiet—'

'Introspective.'

'Yes, that's the word.'

'I think he was lonely. There's not much in the valley for a sensitive, educated man like him. Lonely, and a little frustrated.'

'These last months, he's been another man. Almost...exuberant.'

'It's called happiness, Bill. You can probably remember it if you cast your mind back twenty years.'

'I don't like it when you talk like that, Suse.'

She hugged him. 'I only meant that's how you feel in the first flush, silly.'

'Just so long as she doesn't send him crashing back down to earth, love. It's been plain sailing so far. But the Inspector's upset about this Carstairs kid and when he's upset there's no talking to him sometimes. It's like a shutter comes down in his head. And her, Alison, she's a hard, selfish sort of woman. How will she cope with him then?'

'God, you're unfair sometimes. I like her. Lots of people do. Just because she doesn't fit in with your notion of womanliness. Your notion of womanliness died out in the civilised world in about 1914.'

Bill changed the subject before an argument could develop. 'He sent me home, said he'd be needing me this evening. God knows what for.'

'It's not like him not to tell you what he's up to.'

'Depends how sure he is. If it's one of his more fanciful ideas he often keeps it quiet. Probably just wanted the afternoon off himself.'

'No one in their right mind could accuse Nick Trevellyan of neglecting his duty.'

'Still, we've got a job to do. I mean, we'd all like to spend the afternoon in bed with the missus.'

'Oh, yeah?'

'Well . . . yeah.'

Susie glanced at the clock. 'Just gone two, none of the girls will be home from school until at least four. Or are you all talk?'

Ten minutes later they heard the front door slam and Sarah's voice called, 'It's only me.'

'I'll get rid of her,' Susie said briskly. She put on her dressing gown and went downstairs.

'You're home early, poppet.'

'Well, I always have a free period on Tuesdays and Miss Fielding's off sick so my tutor said I might as well do some private study at home.'

'You've been working very hard lately.' Susie picked up her handbag and took out her purse. 'Give yourself an afternoon off. Here's three quid, go to the pictures or something.'

Sarah stared at her. 'Here,' she said, taking in the dressing gown for the first time, 'have you got a bloke upstairs or something? Because if so, three quid's not enough to buy my silence.'

'Yes, I have got a bloke upstairs as it happens ... your dad.' Susie grinned at her eldest daughter's shocked face, 'So push off and don't come home for at least a couple of hours, OK?'

'We have nurtured a blackmailer in our nest,' she said, as she took the dressing gown off again.

Despite Bill's suspicions, Nick was not similarly employed. In fact he and Alison were up on Threeoaks Hill looking for a man with a greyhound.

Alison had initially demurred at the suggestion of a brisk walk, but she was rather enjoying herself. Her long legs had no difficulty in keeping pace with Nick's purposeful stride.

'Hey, the view's really good from up here,' she exclaimed. 'I can see the sea.'

'I don't know his name, or where he lives,' Nick said. 'Damn it all!'

'The air's so fresh up here,' Alison took in a deep breath.

'I've seen him here lots of times, why the hell isn't he here now?'

'April is my favourite month. Old Eliot didn't know what he was talking about.'

'It's usually in the afternoon. How long should I hang about?'

'Oh, what's that flower?'

'Pink Campion. Don't touch it! If you were brought up in the country you should know not to pick wild flowers.'

'I was only *looking*.'

Nick stopped walking abruptly and turned to her. 'You're not listening to a word I say, Al.'

'Don't call me Al. I rather thought you were talking to yourself.'

'Well, yes,' he said grudgingly, 'doesn't mean you don't have to listen though.' He cupped her cold, flushed face in his hands and kissed it, muttering something about wild geese.

'I leave Bill to follow your babblings, he gets paid for it.' Alison wound her arms round his neck.

'I'm not babbling. I want to see this bloody man.'

'If he knew anything he would have come forward surely.'

'Perhaps he doesn't read the local papers. Perhaps he doesn't even know about the murder.'

'What makes you think he'll be any use?'

'He was up here that afternoon I saw Frisco, the day I got back from my course. Only he was coming away from the copse while I was walking towards it. If she was meeting the same man that afternoon she met on Sunday evening, he might just have seen him.'

'Perhaps it was him.'

'He must be over seventy!'

'OK, perhaps he killed her in a frenzy of jealousy for his lost youth and virility.'

'If you can't be any more helpful than that—'

'If he came from Little Hopford we'd know him, so it stands to reason he comes from Great Hopford. So ask at the post office there.'

'Thank you very much, Watson. I have asked there. I have also asked at the post office in Hopwood and the DSS and the health centre and just about every other bloody place I can think of. No one knows who he is and he's not here now, is he? Come on, let's go home.' He put his arm round her and they retraced their steps back towards Little Hopford.

SEVENTEEN

'WHAT ARE WE DOING HERE, anyway?' Bill grumbled, shuffling about in an attempt to keep warm. 'The SOCOs have been over every inch. It's bloody freezing.'

'I told you to wrap up well,' Nick said unconcernedly.

'What are you expecting to happen up here?'

'Nothing up here. I want to find out why someone thought it worthwhile to scare Molly Armitage off the cliff top. What could she have seen from up here? Give it a few more minutes.'

'There isn't anything to see. Because of the shape of the cliff all you can see from this path is the bay.'

'Precisely.' Nick trained his field glasses out to sea. 'You have a perfect view of one of the quietest bays for miles. Tonight is the start of the dark quarter. You could slip in and out of the Hop Bay without a soul knowing about it on a night like this. You'd feel quite safe until you found out that on old lady was in the habit of walking her dog along the cliff path at night.'

'Only at eleven o'clock. Surely they would wait until a lot later if they were up to no good.'

'Not much later. Not if they had a long way to go. If, say, they had to get all the way over to Ireland.'

'What's in Ireland?'

'A convenient back door into England.'

'But only fishing boats use the bay,' Bill objected. 'It's not as if it's full of ocean-going yachts just waiting to put out to sea.'

'True. They must rendezvous with a bigger boat then, coming the other way. And don't forget the tides. The harbour is dry at low tide and for a couple of hours either side. They couldn't risk putting out any later than eleven-fifteen and five o'clock is the earliest they'll get back in. By five-thirty it will be getting light and the first fishing boats will be putting out.'

Nick turned his back on the bay and trained his pencil-slim torch beam onto his watch. 'Five past eleven now.' He resumed his scrutiny of the bay. After a few minutes he said, 'Yes, I can see movement.'

'Where? I can't see a thing in this dark. Let me have a look through your binoculars... I can just about make out a shape moving out to sea, I think. It's got no lights on.'

'I imagine not. If only there were a few stars in the sky—they've chosen their night well.' Nick took back the binoculars. 'They'll be back at five-fifteen—you could set your watch by them. I think we shall have a little reception committee waiting for that fishing boat when it returns.'

'Does that mean we can go home and come back at quarter to five?' Bill asked hopefully.

'No.'

'Thought not.'

'Get on the car radio. Get Penruan out of whoever's bed he's in tonight; get a couple of constables from the crime squad too, and a couple of dog handlers. I'm not taking any chances. If it's what I think it is they may not come quietly.'

'We should notify Customs and Excise as well,' Bill said doubtfully. 'They'll want to be in on it.'

'We should, yes,' Nick said.

'Yeah.'

'Yeah. Then they can get a helicopter out and waken the dead.'

'Tell them afterwards, then?'

'That's right.'

'The Super won't like it.'

'That's right. Radio in and then we'll pop down to the bay and have a look around. Pity the cliff railway's not working at this time of night, we'll have to go the long way.'

'You wouldn't get me on that thing if you paid me.' Bill got back in the car, started the engine and put the heater full on. Nick got in at the passenger door and opened the window. Bill spent several minutes talking to the radio control room then set off down the steep road to the harbour.

'Leave the car at the foot of the hill,' Nick said. 'We'll walk the rest in case they've got anyone keeping lookout on the shore.' Bill got out and stumbled over a bollard. He swore very quietly.

'You've not been eating up your carrots.' Nick jumped gracefully down into the harbour which seemed quite deserted. They kept their voices to a whisper all the same, as they walked unsteadily across the wet sea strand.

'It lookth much the thame as uthual,' Bill lisped, avoiding hissing sibilants.

'Don't overdo it,' Nick said. 'We're not the secret seven and there's no one else here.'

'I can't see any boats missing,' Bill said, reverting thankfully to normal. 'Surely all the fishing boats are here. Those three belong to the Pugsleys—*Mary Jane* the first, second and third.'

'Yes, imaginative lot.'

'The *White Lady* belongs to Matt Tomkins and the other fishing boats . . . no, they're all there.'

'The fishing boats, yes,' Nick said gravely. 'The only boat which is obviously missing is the *Lorna Doone*.' He glanced at his watch again. 'Nearly midnight.'

'It's going to be a long night,' Bill complained. 'Let's hope someone remembers to bring a pack of cards.'

Nick leant against a rock, put the binoculars away in his bag and produced a flask of coffee to which he had added half a glass of Alison's best brandy when she wasn't looking.

'Drink this and stop moaning,' he instructed. They settled down to wait for reinforcements.

Ten minutes later Nick heard the faintest of footfalls from his right—the landward side. He tensed himself, his hand reaching for a large, sharp piece of loose rock behind him. A voice he knew well said, 'Nick? Is that you?'

'Be a good boy, Kit,' Nick said, turning round, 'and consider yourself under arrest.' Kit moved towards Nick in a gesture which might have been interpreted as threatening. Bill appeared menacingly out of the darkness with a fair turn of speed for a man of his build. Kit held up both hands in a gesture of appeasement.

'Hey,' he said, 'I don't want any trouble. I was just out for a walk and I heard someone moving about and came to investigate. There's been some thefts from boats lately. I wanted to check the *Lorna* was OK.'

'I expect you were just about to call the police,' Nick said. 'Since you must have noticed by now that your boat has gone.'

'None of this is down to me,' Kit said, after a moment's thought.

'None of what, Kit?' Nick asked softly. Kit didn't reply. 'Save it for the interview room,' Nick told him.

NICK REACHED HOPE COTTAGE at nine o'clock the next morning. Alison and Ralph were in the kitchen eating breakfast.

'My darling!' Alison said, getting up. 'You've been out all night. And up all night by the look of you.' Usually he was her darling only when they made love. Nick resolved to stay out all night more often.

'Sorry, my angel. I didn't get a chance to let you know.' He put his arms round her and kissed her. 'I told you right from the start that my work was an even more demanding mistress than you are.'

Ralph sniggered. 'Naughty, naughty, Inspector. Out all night. What a convenient excuse your job must be. What's this week's big crime? Someone been rustling sheep?'

'No, someone slaughtered a lamb,' Nick said. 'Can I have a quick word with you, Alison, in private?'

She followed him down the hall into the sitting room.

'Whatever's up?' she said, mystified. 'Ralph will think you very rude.'

'I daresay. I expect there's something in the Alison Hope etiquette book about not arresting a house guest. I want you to stay here, in fact I'm going to lock you in. I don't know how he'll react—he may be violent.' She stared at him, speechless. 'Tell you all about it later.' Nick planted a quick kiss on her forehead. 'No noise now, that's an order.' He took the key out of the door, turned it on the outside and put it in his pocket.

Bill Deacon and Paul Penruan were now standing, silently, waiting for Nick in the hall. Bill nodded and gave a thumbs-up sign. Nick motioned them to follow him to the kitchen door and they waited there, out of sight, as Nick went in.

'Secrets!' Ralph said. Nick glanced round the room, looking for potential weapons. Ralph was sitting at the breakfast bar. There was a half-full bottle of wine from the previous evening abandoned on the bar in front of him. Nick picked it up and put it in the larder. He took Ralph by the arm and gripped it tightly.

'Here!' Ralph began.

'Ralph Squires, I am arresting you for trafficking in prohibited drugs, following information received. You are not obliged to say anything, but anything you say may be given in evidence.'

Ralph darted a quick look round the room. Bill Deacon and Paul Penruan were now blocking the doorway. He glanced towards the conservatory.

'Try it,' Nick said gleefully. 'I'll have you writhing on the ground before you get two feet. I shall enjoy it.'

'I suppose this is the bit where I say I don't know what you're talking about,' Ralph said calmly.

'If you like.'

'I underestimated you, didn't I, Mr Plod? I'll come quietly, as I believe the expression is.'

Bill handcuffed him and he and Penruan led Ralph out to the police car which was parked out of sight on the grass verge.

Ralph called out, 'Do make my apologies to our charming hostess, Nick. So rude of me to rush off like this. Tell her I had an invitation I simply couldn't refuse.'

'Smartarse!' Nick said. He unlocked the sitting room door.

'OK, Alison. You can come out now.' She was less angry than he had anticipated.

'I just can't believe it,' was all she said when Nick explained.

'It's quite true, I'm afraid. He must have thought it a huge joke staying in a house with a policeman. Well, he's not laughing now.'

'But he's my friend,' she said, shaking her head.

'Yes. And Lynton is my uncle. And it was he who nearly killed Molly Armitage.'

'I suppose Kit was mixed up in it too,' she said when she had digested this information.

'Oddly enough, no. He had more sense than I gave him credit for, and a lot more sense than Lynton. He knew about it but he refused to have anything to do with it. There are various minor things I could charge him with, but I doubt if we'll find it worth the bother.'

'I DIDN'T INTEND to hurt her, Nick. When Ralph told me how she always walked that bloody dog on the cliff at night I knew we'd have to do something about it. She's as sharp as a needle, that woman. I couldn't risk her seeing us putting out to sea. I just wanted to give her a good scare. I knew about that business with the Carstairs kid and I thought if I leapt out and put my hands round her neck that would keep her away at least until the dark quarter was over. Well, I must have been too convincing because she keeled over the minute I touched her and knocked herself out cold on a bit of rock that sticks out just there. The lap dog went bloody berserk and bit me on the hand and I just made myself scarce as quick as I could. No one was more relieved than me when I heard she was all right, I can tell you!'

'Tell me about you and Squires.'

'Well, I met him through you, or at least young Alison. You brought him into the Crow last autumn when he was down here, remember? He saw the potential of the bay at once. He came up one day on his own and started chatting about the coastline. 'Course, I said that I knew these waters like the back of my hand and he said how about a little business deal? All I had to do was rendezvous with the boat out from Waterford on a dark night and bring back some packages. Money for old rope. He said he'd let me know when and where and I didn't hear any more from him until a couple of weeks ago. Then your people cleared up that smuggling ring in Cornwall and he came down. Said this was it and he'd be back for the dark quarter. I was a bit shocked when I realised he was staying at Hope Cottage. I warned him but he just laughed.'

'I could cheerfully kill you, Lynton.'

'You know there's a long tradition of smuggling in the family, boy.'

'Smuggling smack, cocaine—to wreck people's lives?'

'I didn't know what was in the packages,' Lynton said sullenly.

Nick looked at him in disgust. 'What sort of an idiot do you take me for, Lynton? You and Ralph Bloody Squires.'

'I DON'T THINK MUCH OF this hotel,' Ralph said. 'I ordered room service over an hour ago.'

'Keep talking Ralph,' Nick said. 'I've got all day.'

'Look, old man, my solicitor says you can't question me for more than a couple of hours without a break.'

'Did he now?'

'I've told you everything I know about this bloody drug ring, OK?'

'Let's say I believe that for the time being.' Ralph looked relieved. 'So let's talk about something else instead. Let's talk about the murder of Frisco Carstairs.' Ralph stopped looking relieved.

'What!'

'You met her when you were down here in the autumn, picking up your last consignment via the Cornish route. Now, she was in the habit of making overtures to young gentlemen. I don't suppose she left you off her itinerary. And from what I've heard you say about your marriage, and from your attitude to women in general, I have no reason to suppose you turned her down ... Well?'

'All right, so I didn't. That was months ago. I don't know anything about her death. Are you crazy?'

'And now it turns out that you were here, in the valley, the weekend she died. Not in your oh-so-conspicuous Porsche, though. Hired car, was it? You may as well tell me what happened, Ralph. Or shall I tell you? You met Frisco by accident. She recognised you. You realised that she might talk about having seen you down here when you were supposed to be safely in London. So you arranged to meet her that night, drove her up to the copse, screwed her and strangled her.'

Ralph went white. 'No! My God, you must be out of your mind.'

'We'll find out where you hired the car and the forensic people will find traces of Frisco in it—fibres from her clothes, her hairs. So there's no point in lying about it.'

'I'm not. Nick, please! I never saw her again after last autumn. I didn't kill her. You've got to believe me.'

'What blood group are you?'

'Eh? How the hell should I know?'

'We'll take a blood test then and a sperm sample. Where did you hire the car from?'

'Er...'

'Come on. If you've nothing to hide then you've nothing to fear, have you? Did you drive it down from London?'

'No. I got the train to Taunton. I hired the car at a place right outside the station.'

'Did you use your own name?'

'No. I had a false driving licence.'

'Name?'

'Um... Bolton. Clive Bolton.'

'Type and colour of the car?'

'Blue Vauxhall Cavalier.'

'Right. That'd better be the truth.'

'It is.'

'Did you go to public school, Ralph?'

'Yes, why?'

'You won't mind prison so much, then. The public school boys never do. The bullying and the buggery makes them feel at home. Handsome chap like you, still young, you'll be very popular.'

Ralph went even paler. 'I didn't,' he whispered after a moment, 'go to public school.'

'Started lying about our background at Cambridge, did we?' Ralph nodded silently. 'I bet you were dealing in drugs even then.'

Ralph shrugged. 'If it wasn't me it would be some-one else.'

'So you had to invent a monied background to ex-plain being so much richer than the other students, right? Nice family trust fund? Poor little orphaned Ralph? Where do your parents really live, Ralph?'

'Coventry,' he said sullenly. 'As far as I know.'

'Make sure you tell me the whole truth, Ralph. I realise lying is second nature to you but it won't help you now.'

'I am telling the truth.' Ralph looked tiredly at the floor. 'Copse. You said copse. What copse?'

'Threeoaks Copse.'

'You mean that's where the murder happened?'

'You're over-acting Ralph.'

'I had no idea.'

'Why does it worry you so much?'

'It doesn't.'

'OK,' Nick said. 'You can have your break and a meal now. We'll talk some more later—when you've had time to reflect a little on your sins.' They started to take Ralph out.

'Just a minute,' Nick said. 'Who was your contact in London? The next one in the chain.'

'I won't tell you. I'm more frightened of them than I am of you.'

'Oh! I see you really do want to be charged with murder. OK, take him out and charge him.'

'Hang on!' Ralph yelped. 'There wasn't a London contact. It was local.'

'Names, addresses.' Nick said wearily.

'I didn't have an address, just a name and a meeting place.'

'Who and where? Stop wasting my time.'

'Finch. The name is Finch.'

Nick glanced at Bill who shook his head silently. 'When?'

'Dawn tomorrow,' Ralph said reluctantly.

'And the meeting place?' Nick asked, and replied simultaneously with Ralph, 'Threeoaks Copse.'

'Think you know it all, don't you?' Ralph glared at Nick. 'All this fuss over a little no-account slag like that.'

'Get him out of here,' Nick said. 'Before I break both his arms.'

'Do you think he killed Miss Carstairs?' Bill asked when Ralph had gone.

'No, damn it! I don't. He was genuinely taken aback by the location of the body. Get someone to check on that hired car. Apart from that I can't waste any more time on him.'

'This is a bit of bad luck,' Bill said. 'His contact probably won't turn up after what happened.'

'It's beginning to look as if it was very bad luck for Frisco. But if this Finch has no way of contacting Ralph over a change of plan, my bet is he'll turn up. I want today's arrests kept very quiet indeed. I'll have a word with Kit and Lorna to make sure they keep their mouths shut. Get the copse unsealed immediately. When we have Finch, we may well have our murderer.' Nick glanced at his watch. 'I'm going home for a couple of hours for a meal and a bath and I suggest you do the same. Just as soon as you've made the arrangements for dawn tomorrow.'

Nick wanted to wash the foul taste of Ralph out of his mouth. And he needed a hug from Alison very badly.

EIGHTEEN

'BUT NICK SAID I could take the afternoon off,' Paul Penruan protested, as Carol brought the car to a halt in front of the church. 'I was up most of the night. They don't half pick some times to bleep a bloke.'

'Don't be so lazy,' Carol said. 'There's still a few questions need answering.'

'Feel free to ask them without me,' Paul grumbled, but he got out of the car and followed Carol up Church Path. 'What makes you think old man Lawson knows anything?'

'I told you, I saw him hanging about the copse early this morning. I call that dead suspicious.'

'I don't.'

'It's still sealed off.'

'Even an old lag can take a walk over the moors, Carrie. What were you doing there?'

'I couldn't get to sleep with you out God-knows-where so I went for a walk over the moors.'

'See.'

'Shh. Here we are.' Carol knocked loudly on the door of number three. Sam opened the door and looked at them indifferently.

'Hello, Sam,' Carol said. 'Do you remember me? Detective Constable Halsgrove?'

'I'm not senile yet. I remember you all right.' He glanced contemptuously at Penruan. 'Who's this? Your kid sister?'

'DC Penruan,' Carol said politely.

'Taking pretty boys in the force now, aren't they?' Sam said with a sneer. 'Charm the villains down off the trees, does he?'

'I'd like to ask you a few questions.' Carol put her foot in the door.

'I've already told Mr High-And-Mighty Trevellyan everything I know—namely nothing.'

'All the same.'

'Oh, all right.' Sam caved in suddenly. 'The sooner you come in, the sooner you'll bugger off and leave me in peace.' He stepped back with this gracious invitation and Carol and Paul went into the house.

'You were up at the copse this morning,' Carol said. 'You were seen.'

'Oh, yeah? Has catching rabbits been made illegal since I was last out then?' Sam suddenly whipped a ferret from his pocket and thrust it into Carol's face. Penruan took a step back with a cry of disgust. Carol stood her ground.

'Lively little fellow, isn't he?' she said. 'My dad kept ferrets. Vicious little creatures, though. You shouldn't shove them in people's faces like that.'

Sam grinned suddenly. 'I like you. You've got guts, girl, for all this old timer's practically toothless. You should have found yourself a better job. Yeah, I was there this morning and a lot of mornings and I was looking for rabbits, like I said. I'm fond of a bit of rabbit pie. You never get that sort of grub in the nick, you know? Proper English country grub. Besides some of the restaurants'll take them if I can get enough. Getting posh now, rabbit stew, only they call it *casserole de lapin*.' The dish would not have been recognised anywhere from Calais to Nice the way Sam pronounced it.

'The copse is a good place,' he went on. 'Only it's still shut off. I dunno. Took you lot long enough to get up there in the first place and now you're gonna keep it closed 'til Christmas, I shouldn't wonder.'

'Rubbish!' Carol said, stung. 'Mrs Swift found the body at nine o'clock and we had the place sealed off by twenty to ten. I don't call that slow.'

'Nine o'clock!'

'Yes,' Carol said patiently. 'And it took her twenty minutes to get home and raise the alarm.'

Sam began to laugh. 'It was about half-past seven when I saw her going into the copse with that nervous labrador of hers. I should ask her why she took so long reporting it, if I was you.'

WHEN NICK GOT BACK to Hope Cottage, Dot was there, giving the hall floor a good thrashing.

'Hello, Dot,' he said diffidently. 'Glad you're back.'

'Yeah, well,' she said. 'You're just doing your job, aren't you?' She stopped giving the floorboards what for and leant on her broom. 'Fact is, you were right decent to my Ben.'

'How is he?'

'Not too bad. I have to admit he really was keen on the girl. He'll get over it. Sam's been very good with him. Funny thing, that, Sam always seemed to like Ben best of all the kids.' Dot shook her head at the endless idiocies of human nature where a man might love another man's bastard as his own child. 'As for Alan, he only got what he deserved.'

'Ah,' Nick temporised, having no right to discuss Alan Lawson's failings, even with his mother. 'You heard about that?'

'Angela came to see me. She was in a right state. Brought the two kiddies—first time they've been let over to my place, allowed to see their grandpa. It's an ill wind...'

'Angela confided in you?' Nick said, astonished.

'She's got no mother of her own,' Dot explained. 'She's not about to pour it all out to her dad, is she? So she came to me. She's not so bad. Better than he deserves, if you ask me.'

'Give him another chance, Dot,' Nick said. He didn't add that she hadn't exactly been the best example of marital fidelity.

'You men,' Dot said, rigorously applying her own double standards. 'All stick together. Bit on the side, eh? Who cares? Oh, I can see what you're thinking,' she added shrewdly. 'It's not my place to cast the first stone, right? Well, for your information Lynton wasn't a bit on the side. I loved that rotten sod.'

'I'm sorry, Dot.' Nick wasn't sure what he was sorry for—whatever it was Uncle Lynton had done to qualify him as such a rotten sod or the news of his arrest which was bound to hit Dot in a day or two.

'Besides,' Dot went on as if he hadn't spoken, 'I like working for Alison. Not just because she pays me better than the others either. She's a proper lady. She knows how to treat a charlady, not like some of them—either overbearing or all over you. She wants her money's worth, OK, but she's always very fair. You know where you are with Alison.'

'Mmm,' said Nick, who sometimes wished he did.

'Have you heard? Sam's got a job at the dairy, starting Monday.'

'That's wonderful. Doing what?'

'Oh you know, fetching and carrying, lifting things.'

'Make sure he doesn't "lift" anything.'

'Very humorous,' Dot said sourly. 'Remind me to laugh some time.'

Nick went off in search of Alison.

'DO YOU WANT me to call him at home?' the radio reserve crackled. 'Receiving. Over.'

'No, it's all right,' Carol said. 'We're in Little Hopford ourselves. Out.' She replaced the radio handset.

'The boss has gone home,' she said. 'We'll just have to disturb him, that's all.'

'Hope Cottage, here we come.' Penruan started the engine and shot out of the lay-by without signalling. Carol closed her eyes. 'Try not to hit anything.'

Paul screeched the car to a halt in the courtyard about three minutes later. Dot Lawson opened the door almost at once and glared at them as they got out of the car.

'Who d'you think you are?' she asked Paul. 'One of Rockliffe's bleeding babies?'

'Is the Inspector in please, Mrs Lawson?' Carol asked.

'Mr Trevellyan's in the garden with Miss Hope. I don't know that they want to be disturbed.'

'Would you tell him we're here, please?' Carol said. 'We wouldn't disturb him at home if it wasn't important.'

'Oh, all right,' Dot said, suitably pacified. 'Come in. Wipe your feet. I've just done the hall floor.'

She stood over them while they obeyed her instruction with exaggerated care then led them through the drawing room out on to the terrace. Nick and Alison were sitting on a bench under the pear tree. At least Alison was sitting on it; Nick was stretched out along it with his head in her lap. Carol could hear the faint murmur of their voices—low and caressing. She hesitated. Paul had no such scruples.

'Hey, boss!' he called. Nick sat up in surprise. He said something to Alison, who laughed and shrugged. Then he got up and walked resignedly across the lawn towards them. He stood at the foot of the terrace steps looking at them questioningly. His hair was damp and he smelt faintly of horse chestnuts. Both Paul and Carol began talking at once.

'We're sorry to disturb you, sir,' Carol said while Paul said, 'You're never gonna believe this, boss.'

'Stop!' Nick said. 'We'll go upstairs to the study where we can talk privately.' Paul and Carol realised that Dot was still standing behind them on the terrace cocking an interested ear. They both blushed. 'And one of you can tell me about it without the Greek chorus,' Nick went on. They followed him up the stairs.

'Sorry, sir,' Carol said when they were safely closeted in Alison's study. 'Only we were so excited.'

'You tell me, Carol. I don't think I can bear Paul's hyperbolic prose style at the moment.'

Carol recounted their interview with Sam Lawson as briefly as possible.

'Swift!' Nick said when she'd finished. 'Finch!' Seeing their puzzled looks he explained. 'Not a very inventive alias. I'm being stupid today.'

'You were up all night,' Carol pointed out.

'Even so. Which reminds me, I told you to go home, Paul.'

'It was Paul's idea,' Carol said. Paul looked steadfastly out of the window, a satisfied smile flickering across his face. 'It struck him that Sam Lawson often hung about on the moors, rabbiting. He asked me to come and help him.'

'You're no use to me worn out, Paul,' Nick said kindly. 'So next time I tell you to go home and catch up on some sleep, do as I say, okay?' He clapped the young man on the back. 'Well done!' Paul blushed with becoming modesty.

'What now?' Carol asked.

'I think our best bet is still to catch her red-handed,' Nick said. 'After all Squires doesn't know her real name and it was dark last time he met her. She may well not have any drugs in her house at the moment either. If we descend on Old Mill House with a search warrant and arrest her now we might find ourselves laughed out of court.'

'Can we come?' Carol asked.

'Oh, yes. You're both marked down for this little excursion all right. Dawn tomorrow. Shoot home now, both of you, and meet me at base at half-past four.'

'YOU DIDN'T HAVE TO do that, Carrie,' Paul said when they were safely back in their car.

'I didn't have to, no. I wanted to.'

'Thanks. Just in time for my annual report, as it happens. Give us a kiss.'

'Not here, dummy. You know the guv'nor's rules.'

'What?' Paul said, startled. Carol stared at him in surprise.

'He doesn't allow...romantic...entanglements on his team. Surely you knew?'

'I had no idea,' Paul said, in horror.

'There was a couple at HQ, screwed up a surveillance operation because they were too engrossed in each other. That's the only time I've seen Nick really blow his top. Good job we're not armed in this country otherwise I think they'd both just have gone out and shot themselves.'

'That doesn't sound like him.'

'When he gets angry with you, you'll know about it. In fact, you'll probably curl up and die.'

'So what happens if he finds out?'

'He'll make one of us transfer.'

'Great,' Paul said slowly. 'Really great. As if I didn't know which one of us it would be.'

'He may have revised his ideas a bit since he met Alison. He knows now what it's like to love someone so much you don't care what risks you take for them. I don't think he's ever felt like that about anyone before. Don't worry about it.'

Paul frowned as he started the engine. It was beginning to look as if he'd scored an own goal.

NINETEEN

IT WAS STILL five minutes before sunrise when a cracking of twigs at the stile betrayed the arrival of Penelope Swift. She picked her way across the copse, muttering occasionally to herself or possibly to the dog.

'Thank God they opened the place up again, Labby,' Nick heard her say when she was in earshot. 'I don't know what we would have done otherwise. Hmm. Eh, sweetheart?' Labby wagged her tail. Mrs Swift examined her watch in the twilight and glanced round nervously.

'Mr Knightley?' she called softly. 'Are you there?'

Squires, Nick thought, Knightley. No, they didn't go very far for their aliases. Nobody moved. Mrs Swift sat down on a tree stump and scuffled her feet in the leaves. Labby ran off into the bushes, ignoring her mistress's call.

'Labby! Come back here, you silly girl. What's the matter with you?'

The sun rose over Little Hopford and came filtering through the network of branches into the heart of the copse. Paul Penruan who, like Ralph, was tall and blond, stepped out from behind a clump of bushes with the sun behind him. Mrs Swift started up.

'Thank goodness. I thought you might not come with the fuss there's been around this place.' She screwed up her eyes against the light. 'Have you got it?' Penruan nodded. 'Don't let's hang about, for Christ's sake.'

Penruan advanced into the shadow of an oak and held out a plastic carrier bag innocuously emblazoned with the name of a well-known supermarket chain. She snatched it from him and took out one of the packets. She opened it, licked her finger, stuck it in the bag like a child with a lemon sherbert and pressed the white powder to her tongue. Her hands shook as she counted the packets clumsily.

'All right?' Penruan said in an unidentifiable whisper.

She nodded. 'Right. Get out of here and out of the valley at once. I'll give you ten minutes before I go home myself.'

'I don't think you'll be going home for quite a while, Mrs Swift,' Nick said from behind her. She froze. From every side bodies appeared from nowhere to encircle her. Labby continued to ignore her mistress, who smelt only of fear, in favour of the dog handler who smelt, more enticingly, of aniseed. Penelope Swift turned slowly, her frightened eyes darting round the ring, taking in the faces as the sun penetrated more surely through the branches. Bill Deacon, placid, watchful; Paul Penruan, arms folded, expectant, an almost-amused smile on his face; two constables with school-boy complexions, a little nervous at their first big arrest; Nick Trevellyan, a tired-eyed avenging angel; Carol Halsgrove, exultant and implacable. She looked for the weakest link and bolted. She chose badly. Carol, five feet four and built like a ballet dancer, sent her crashing to the ground at the foot of the tallest oak. She lay, helpless with Carol's knee in her back. Nick crouched down beside her.

'You recognise this oak tree, Penelope? Of course it was very dark that night but this is the place where you strangled little Frisco. Remember? Remember how you grabbed both ends of her scarf and pulled. Do you feel helpless now? How helpless did she feel, d'you think?'

Penelope Swift began to scream.

'Why did you do it, Penelope? Was she black-mailing you? Or were you merely afraid that she might? What did she see? What did she find?'

'No!' Penelope screamed. 'It wasn't me. I only found her.'

At a nod from Nick, Carol dragged Mrs Swift back to her feet. Bill helped to hold her up since she seemed unable to stand.

'Penelope Swift, you are under arrest,' Nick said. 'You will be taken to Hopbridge police station where you will be charged with drug trafficking and murder.' He began to caution her.

'No!' she screamed, drowning his words. 'It isn't true. Not murder. No!'

'THANK GOODNESS Nick arrested that awful Squires boy,' Molly said. 'You really are the most appalling judge of character, Alison.'

'He never used to be like that,' she protested feebly.

'He must have been. You don't get as obnoxious as that overnight. I'm sorry about Lynton though. I always liked him.'

'Did you know it was he who attacked you?'

'No, but Castlemaine didn't raise the alarm until I was actually attacked, implying that the attacker was someone she knew. She reacts quite differently to strangers—barks her head off the minute she sets eyes on them. I really didn't think of Lynton for a moment.'

'Nick's gone very quiet since he arrested him. If only he wouldn't bottle it all up so. I mean, who can he talk to if not to me?'

'Mmm. It's never been easy to tell what was going on inside Nick Trevellyan's head.'

'He also got an idea that Ralph might have killed Frisco. He can't find a scrap of evidence to prove it—rather the contrary. So he's very annoyed about that. He really fancied Ralph for the role of The Strangler.'

'I can see one would be tempted. Tell me, what did Nick's father do?'

'He was a school teacher, so was his mother.'

'Never mind about her,' Molly said, dismissing Nick's mother with a wave of her hand. 'An oddly assorted family, the Trevellyans.'

'Nick said once that his father was quite eccentric. I think Lynton was the youngest of the family and rather left to run wild.'

'Are there any more of them?'

'There was another brother, that's Margaret Lohitzun's father, and a sister, that's Avis from the Health Centre.'

'Ghastly woman.'

'Yes, she is. Don't let's talk about her. Talk about something pleasant.'

'Speaking of the Health Centre, will Ned Savage marry Lorna now, d'you think?'

'I suppose it depends how deeply she's got her hooks into him.'

Molly pursed her lips. 'He's an ambitious young man. He won't take kindly to the idea of a jailbird for a father-in-law. My bet is he'll break off the engagement.'

'Oh well, Lorna will no doubt sell his ring for a tidy sum and start the hunt all over again.'

'Is that the way of it?'

'I think so.'

'Poor silly girl,' Molly said. 'To marry a man she doesn't love.'

'I think she looks on it as a good career move. Ned won't get such a bad bargain if he sticks to her. She'll keep her side of it.' Alison leant back comfortably in her chair and smiled to herself. Molly looked fondly at her goddaughter, so relaxed and happy.

'You're very different from last year, Alison. When you moved down here, after all that hard living in London, you were…brittle, as if you might fall at any moment and shatter into pieces on the ground. Now you're just the opposite. The air of the Hop Valley has got into you.'

'Nick's got into me, more like.'

'No need to be crude!' Molly giggled suddenly. 'Still I suppose that was what I meant really. You have that infuriatingly smug expression of a woman who is being kissed hard and often and by someone who knows how.' Alison laughed in delight. 'So when are you two getting married? You can tell me to mind my own business, of course…but then you'll get a pot of Earl Grey poured over your head.'

'We're not,' Alison said.

'What! Don't tell me he hasn't asked you.'

'A dozen times at least.'

'And you said no? You silly little girl.'

'We're just fine as we are. You know I have a phobia about marriage, Molly.'

'I don't know anything of the sort. All I know is that you never met the right man before.'

'You never did like Gareth, did you?'

'Alison, *nobody* liked Gareth, except you.'

'I'm not sure that I *liked* him very much. Certainly not at the end.'

'The man was a boor. Don't fall into the trap of judging all men by him.'

'Was that boor or bore or Boer?'

'All of those.'

Alison laughed. 'Jan says if you meet a man who doesn't get on your nerves more than once a week, you should hang on to him.'

'Last of the great romantics, Ms Baxter,' Molly said. 'I shall have a word with Nick Trevellyan and tell him he's got to put his foot down.'

'Don't you dare.'

'I don't know why he lets you get away with it. If he said marriage or nothing, you'd be out buying your wedding dress before you could say Harrods Bridal Department. Admit.'

'Maybe. All right, I expect so. But he won't say it, so I'm quite safe.'

'You may fool everyone else, Alison Hope, with your bossy ways but you don't fool me. I've known you since you were two weeks old. You like to think you rule the roost, whereas the truth is that he'd only have to snap his fingers to bring you to heel—if he but knew it.' Molly snapped her fingers in demonstration and Castlemaine launched into an orgy of barking.

'Shut up, you,' Molly said. 'It's not time for walkies. All right, Alison, you can take that homicidal look off your face. I won't tell him. But remember: "If you will not while you may, when you will you shall have nay".'

'Who cares about that stupid little slag?' Penny Swift asked Nick.

'I do,' he replied calmly.

'People like her, useless parasites. Hanging around the villages all day; producing nothing, creating nothing. My father...'

'What?' Nick asked after a pause. Penny Swift was slumped low in her chair, a frightened child. 'What would your father have done?'

'Would have beaten some sense into her,' she replied quietly. She hugged her arms close around her. 'He couldn't stand idleness, wastefulness, people who... didn't achieve anything... Failures... People who came second.'

'Yes,' Nick said slowly. 'I see.'

'And she was pregnant too, another half-witted brat for the tax payer to bring up. Why didn't they sterilise her when she reached puberty? Tell me that. Same with drug addicts—why should I care about them? Why shouldn't I make a bit of money out of them? If I don't someone else will. How are we supposed to live these days? Decent people like us? Taxes, school fees, rates...'

'Frisco was a human being, a person, gentle, harmless.' Nick stared at her with dismay and with half-reluctant pity.

'Parasites!' she repeated vehemently.

'You knew Frisco was pregnant? You killed her because of that?'

'Of course I didn't,' she said in disgust. 'I wouldn't soil my hands.'

'She used to hang around Threeoaks Copse at night. She could easily have seen you picking up one of your drug consignments.'

'She wouldn't have had the sense to know what it meant. If she had and had tried to blackmail me, I might have had a bit of respect for her. I never saw her there. I didn't know she used the place. I didn't kill her. I'd hardly kill her there anyway. The idea was to keep people away from the place not get hundreds of flat-foot coppers trampling over it.'

'Why did you take so long reporting finding the body—if it wasn't you who killed her?'

'I've just said. I knew it would mean your people swarming over the place so I had to make sure there was nothing incriminating for them to find. I even toyed with the idea of moving her somewhere else but I had no transport and she was a lot heavier than I expected—dead weight—and stiff too.' She shuddered in distaste. 'Besides I knew you probably wouldn't be fooled. I've seen those programmes on the television—forensic medicine and stuff. I tidied up, I may have moved her a bit. I didn't kill her. Do I look like a murderer?'

'You murder only at one remove,' Nick said softly. 'You don't see the drug addicts dying in the public lavatories, not in Hopbridge. Try Piccadilly Circus late at night, Mrs Swift, or St Paul's in Bristol. Take a look at those teenagers with their needles and then tell me you're not a murderer.'

'I didn't kill the Carstairs brat,' she repeated.

'I'm going to take a lot of convincing, Penelope.'

But Nick believed her. Just as he believed Ralph. He could have made out a case against either one of them. But what would be the point of that? He wanted a murderer, not an arrest.

'I'LL BE GLAD to have Sophie back tomorrow,' Molly said. 'I see so little of her.'

'Oh my God!' Alison said.

'Forgotten you'd invited her to dinner, I suppose. She won't mind being put off.'

'I wouldn't dream of it. I'd love to have a nice long talk with her.'

'I can't think why, you haven't got a thing in common. And I must say, the things she comes out with sometimes ... You'd never think her father used to be a diplomat, would you?'

'I simply can't imagine where she gets it from,' Alison replied sarcastically. 'What I meant was that it was Nick who invited her and you can bet your last pound he won't be there.'

TWENTY

'I'M GOING TO let you go now, Kit,' Nick said. 'But you and I are going to have a long talk very soon.'

'What will happen to Dad?' Kit asked.

'Ask the judge.'

'Nick, there's something I've been meaning to talk to you about. About Frisco.'

Nick looked at him sharply. 'I hope this isn't going to be a confession.'

'No! I heard something one night recently, in the Dog and Duck in West Hopbridge.'

'And what were you doing in that dive? Buying marijuana, I suppose.'

Kit went scarlet. 'How did you know?'

'I can see it in your eyes, boy.'

'It's harmless,' Kit said sullenly. 'They should make it legal.'

'Whether I agree with that or not is completely irrelevant.'

'Look, do you want to hear what I heard, or not?'

'I'm listening.'

'They were talking about her, Frisco, laughing, saying she asked for it. Don't look at me like that, Nick, I'm just repeating what they were saying.'

'Go on.'

'Then one of them said how he'd seen her with the Lawson bloke a dozen times in the past few months. Then he laughed and said something like, "I'm not going to shop him—if it hadn't been him it'd have been someone else. Let the pigs go on chasing their own tails.'' Then someone nudged him and nodded towards me and he shut up.'

'You being such a well-known law-abiding citizen?'

'Me being your cousin.'

'When was this?'

'Three, four days ago.'

'And it didn't occur to you to come and tell me about it before?'

'No,' Kit said simply. 'Not my business.'

'Who is this man?' Nick asked, struggling to keep his temper.

'No idea. I've seen him there a few times.'

'Don't his friends call him anything?'

'John. His name's John.'

'Are you taking the piss, Kit?'

'No.'

'Well that narrows it down to a few hundred men in the valley, assuming he's local and doesn't just come here to sell dope to gullible boys who ought to know better. How old is he?'

Kit shrugged. 'Forty?'

'Don't make any plans for tonight, Kit. I want you at the Dog and Duck at, shall we say, nine o'clock. OK?'

'OK.'

'And do yourself a favour and lay off the dope.'

'OK,' Kit said sulkily.

'Did you ever sleep with her?' Nick asked.

'Once or twice,' Kit said warily.

Nick sighed. 'I expect you're blood group O, aren't you? Same as me.'

'Yeah. Oh, I get it. Not recently—it must have been eighteen months ago at least.'

'Why did you?' Nick asked curiously. To his surprise Kit flared up in anger.

'Not everyone's had what you've had, Nick,' he blurted out. 'A close, loving family. You never had to watch Uncle George and Aunt Hannah tear each other to pieces the way Mum and Dad did.'

'I didn't know,' Nick said slowly. He remembered Aunt Betty as a dim, pale creature who wouldn't have said boo to a goose.

'He was carrying on with Dot Lawson years before Mum died—don't let either of them tell you different. Everyone thinks what a good guy he is—they don't have to live with him. Why do you think Lorna is so desperate to escape? I'm glad he's shown himself in his true colours at last. Now everyone will know what he was really like and we shall be free of him at last, me and Lorna.'

Nick said nothing. He couldn't think of anything to say. After a moment Kit went on more calmly. 'Your parents gave you everything: education, ambition, principles...love. The ability to make something of your life. Uncle George never told you you were stupid and useless, did he? Well, you weren't. And now you've got Alison. Oh, I know everyone says you're an ill-matched couple and it won't last—'

'Who's everyone?' Nick said, stung.

'Everyone,' Kit replied unhelpfully. 'But it isn't true, is it? It's as if both of you, all your lives, you were just waiting for each other. You never needed to run off after someone like Frisco. Why should you? You don't need to give yourself the illusion that someone cares about you for a few minutes...' Kit ground to a halt and collapsed, deflated.

'I don't really know what to say,' Nick said.

'I've just been bottling it up for so long.'

'I'll say! Do you really resent me so much?'

'Not you,' Kit muttered. 'It's not you I resent.'

'There's only one person can make anything of your life, Kit, and that's you—Christopher Trevellyan.'

'Yeah! Yeah. How long will Dad go away for?'

'I told you, I don't know.'

'A few years?'

'Quite possibly.'

'Good,' Kit said.

'BUT WHICH LAWSON BLOKE?' Bill asked.

'I think we know that,' Nick said.

'Just remind me though.'

'This John said the last few months—that rules out Sam. Kit says he's about forty—I think if he meant Ben he would have said "the Lawson boy" not "the Lawson bloke". Besides Ben had no reason to hide his friendship with Frisco. So that leaves—'

'Bingo!' Bill said gleefully.

'You may as well say it and get it off your chest.'

'I told you so.'

'Good. Feeling better?'

'Yes.'

'Remember his blood group doesn't match the samples?'

'Oh…bother! Let's haul him in anyway. It could still be his kid. He might have killed her out of jealousy if he caught her with someone else that night.'

Nick pondered. 'Hearsay evidence at the moment. If he keeps his head and sticks to his story—'

'He's the nervous type. I don't reckon he'll keep his head—not if we tell him we *know* he's been seeing her.'

'We'll pick him up tonight, after we've been to the Dog and Duck.'

'You think this John will repeat his story to you?' Bill asked doubtfully. 'He doesn't exactly qualify as public-spirited citizen of the year.'

'No, although we've got quite a bit of leverage we can use on him. But at that time of night, it'll take longer to get hold of a solicitor to keep Lawson's head for him.'

IT WAS ONE A.M. and Alan Lawson would not budge. Nick was beginning to have more respect for the man.

'It isn't true,' Alan said for the umpteenth time. 'I've seen her only once in the last year and that was the time I told you about, when I bought her a drink.'

'Your blood group doesn't match the sperm found in her,' Nick reminded him. 'So why are you so afraid to admit to having an affair with her recently, Alan, to admit that the baby might be yours?'

'Don't keep calling me "Alan". I know your game, Trevellyan and I won't stand for it. You were probably screwing her yourself. God knows, you had the best opportunity of anyone.'

Nick stared at him steadily with the penetrating look which convinced the more nervous criminals that he could see into their souls and that lying to him was a waste of breath. Alan Lawson's soul was shrouded in fog.

'My wife's moved into the spare room,' he said wretchedly. 'She's talking of leaving altogether. It's all your fault. I hate you, Trevellyan. Can't you see you're ruining my life? You're too fucking incompetent to find the real murderer, so you have to screw my life up instead.' He leant back wearily in his chair. 'You can't just keep me here for hours like this.'

'It's been two hours, Alan,' Nick said. 'We'll take a short break soon, then we'll go on.'

'I haven't seen her. I didn't kill her. You can keep me here and bully me all night, I'm not going to say anything different.'

Nick glanced at his watch. They would have to let Lawson take a rest in a minute and time was running short. He was probably at his most vulnerable now; more tired than he had been two hours ago and no less frightened. Time to play the ace.

'The thing is, Alan,' he said smoothly, 'that I've got a witness. A witness who saw you and Miss Carstairs together several times recently.'

Alan gaped at him. 'All right!' he said unexpectedly. 'Let's see him then, this witness. Let's hear him accuse me to my face.'

'All in good time,' Nick said, poker-faced, for there had been no sign of "John" at the Dog and Duck.

There was a tap at the door and the custody sergeant put his head round and made an obscene gesture with his hand which Nick interpreted as meaning that the duty solicitor had finally arrived. He got up and followed the sergeant out into the corridor. Bill pulled up a chair and sat down next to Alan.

'We've got a witness, Mr Lawson,' he said gently, 'like Mr Trevellyan says. Better to get it off your chest, eh? Make a new statement. You'll feel better then and you can go home...maybe...and have a nice rest. I—'

Alan said very slowly and distinctly: 'Get stuffed.'

Nick came back a few minutes later with the custody sergeant trotting at his heels.

'Well, he's had a wasted journey,' Nick was saying. 'I'm not holding Mr Lawson any longer. You can let him go.'

'Sir!' Dave Appleby wished the CID glamour boys would make their bloody minds up.

'IT DOESN'T WORK SO WELL these days,' Bill said gloomily. 'The old good-cop, bad-cop routine. He didn't budge.'

'They've all seen it done on TV,' Nick said. 'They don't fall for it any more.'

'Can I be bad-cop one day?' Bill asked.

'You've got the wrong face for it,' said Nick who wanted the role for himself. 'You need a thin, mean-looking bastard like me. You look far too avuncular.'

'Huh!' Bill was not deceived. 'I didn't think he'd have the guts to stick to his story, you know. I thought he'd be the sort who'd break down and confess—be *glad* to confess, relieved.'

Nick nodded. 'I didn't think his nerve would hold up so well. I thought if he really knew more than he was letting on, he'd be in such paroxysms of guilt, he'd blurt the whole lot out. Well, let's hope Carol and Paul can dredge up this "John" tomorrow. Go home now, Bill, and I don't want to see you here before ten to-morrow.'

'You take your own advice,' Bill said.

'I intend to, m'dear. I intend to.'

ALISON STIRRED SLIGHTLY when Nick got into bed. She turned over and put her arms round him without waking up. He fell quickly asleep and slept, hardly moving, for nearly eight hours. When he awoke he was still cradled in her arms and she was watching him, smiling. He yawned and stretched.

'Quarter to nine,' she said, anticipating his first question. 'I was just beginning to wonder if I ought to wake you.'

'You must have been awake for hours.'

'I don't mind watching you sleep, listening to you muttering.'

'What did I say? The name of Frisco's murderer dredged up from my subconscious?'

'Nothing so coherent. Is it in your subconscious?'

'Perhaps. Probably not.'

She ran her fingers lightly down his spine.

'Gotta get up,' he murmured.

'In a minute.'

'Gotta get up in a minute,' he agreed.

Their coupling was sleepy and languid and none the less sweet for that; Alison's orgasm a violin solo rather than the full orchestra crescendo. For once she eschewed her raucous shouts of encouragement and, much as Nick normally enjoyed the frank enthusiasm which had raised a few eyebrows over breakfast at hotels they had stayed at (so that was the couple in room 12!), he was grateful this morning for her instinctive gentle restraint. Afterwards he lay quietly for some minutes, still inside her, unwilling to separate, wanting his body to be absorbed into hers. He loved her best in the early morning—before she put her company director's armour on.

'Nice,' she whispered as they finally drew apart. 'Very nice, my darling.'

'I feel ready to face another day now,' Nick said. 'In a minute.' He told her about the conversation Kit had overheard in the Dog and Duck.

'It would be nice if it was Alan,' she said.

Nick laughed. 'My job would be so much easier if every time a crime was committed, I just charged the most unpleasant person to hand,' he agreed.

'Aren't all crimes committed by unpleasant people?'

'Nearly all. Occasionally they're committed by people who're weak or silly or desperate and the more awful the crime, the more likely that is to be the case. Inadequate people don't rob banks but they do commit murder, rape, child abuse—and now I must get up. Absolutely this very minute.'

'I suppose you've forgotten that Sophie is coming to dinner tonight.'

'I hadn't, funnily enough. I suppose it's my turn to cook supper, strictly speaking.'

'It has been for the last ten days,' Alison agreed amiably.

'Well, if Sophie will settle for a Tandoori take-away—'

'She would but I shan't.'

'I'll put in a fortnight's cooking duty when I've made an arrest, all right?'

'So are we to be honoured by your presence this evening, Detective Inspector?'

'I shall be home by seven. Mmm, that's nice.'

'Promise?'

'I promise. In fact, if you keep on doing that, I'm prepared to promise never to leave the house again.'

'Breakfast,' Alison said sternly, sliding out of bed. 'Ten minutes. Be there.'

TWENTY-ONE

ALISON STOOD on the pavement in Sheep Street at lunchtime staring into the butcher's window, absorbed in the relative merits of different kinds of duck. She knew Sophie didn't care what she ate, didn't even notice but she, Alison, cared very much. A shrill voice hailed her from the end of the street and she froze in horror. It was Avis Trevellyan. She snarled into the plate glass, much to the surprise and dismay of the butcher who took it as a comment on his wares and began to examine his sausages vigorously. Perhaps they were a little past their best. Alison composed her features into something approaching a smile and turned around. Avis was scuttling up the street as fast as her bulk would allow. Alison opened her mouth to say "Hello" but Avis, still some yards away, had already plunged straight in.

'Oh, Alison,' she began. 'How lucky to...' Avis's technique was never to draw breath at the end of a sentence, only in the middle, making it impossible to interrupt her without seeming rude.

'...run into you. So lucky. Have you heard about Lorna? Isn't it exciting? Such a nice man. And a doctor too. I was over the moon when she told me. When I got to work today I just had to kiss him, after all I'll soon be his aunt. He looked so startled when I said that. I don't think it had occurred to...' Alison grinned, picturing Ned Savage's reaction to this prospect.

'...him. His aunt. And Lorna's so full of it all. It's going to be next month which seems rather soon but she isn't pregnant. Oh dear me no! And I won't have...anyone saying that she is after all when a young couple are so...much in love what's the point in delaying, and she'll look so lovely in white with her dark colouring and orange...blossoms in her hair, she says, and a reception at the Pheasant so very...' Alison reflected that the only person likely to start spreading rumours that Lorna was pregnant was Avis herself.

'...smart. I can just see her walking up the aisle of St Stephen's on Lynton's arm and him still so good-looking and distinguished—for his age.' Alison said nothing. She could hardly tell Avis that this particular scene of her fantasy, if not the whole of it, was now out of the question. But Avis didn't expect any reply, indeed left no space for one. Her pudgy face flushed unbecomingly. 'She's got no mother, do you think she'll ask me to act as the bride's mother? That would be nice. There's Meg, of course, she's married but she's only a cousin—it's not the same as an aunt and no children of her own, the poor love. Lorna might ask Meg. I do so hope she asks me.'

Alison murmured something incomprehensible.

'Nick will bring you, of course,' Avis smiled coyly. 'Spring is such a nice time for a wedding, I always say.'

'Quite,' Alison slipped in.

'The engagement is announced in the paper today too.' Avis began to rummage through her capacious shopping bag. 'Now where did I put it. I must show you. Such a nice photo of Nick at the inquest too. Oh, how stupid I am. I gave the paper to Jean-Luc to show to Meg. I'll have to buy another. I ran into him in the...market. He was buying something very odd, what was it? Fennel? He's such a nice man, terribly lugubrious, of course, but such a good husband to Meg—for a foreigner. I had such a job making him understand what I was saying and of course I can hardly understand a word *he* says.' She laughed. Alison wondered how she knew since she presumably never let Jean-Luc get a word in edgeways. 'He can read English a lot better than he speaks it so I showed him the announcement. I think he said he'd make them a cake. Isn't that lovely?'

Alison, who by now felt as if she was being drowned in a huge butt of verbal malmsey, merely nodded dumbly.

IT WAS ONLY half-past six when Nick's car lurched uncertainly into the courtyard that evening. Alison met him in the front hall.

'Oh good, you're early. I've just had Sophie on the phone. Anton's been delayed and can't bring her over and Molly is still too woozy to drive. I said one of us would go and fetch her. Will you?'

'Yes, of course.'

She took a set of keys from a hook by the door. 'Take the Jag. Sophie doesn't want to be chauffeured round the valley in your heap.'

'I suppose I shall have to. There's something wrong with my car. The engine's making a terrible racket.'

'That makes a change.'

'We'll have less of your cheek.' Nick put his arms round Alison's waist and drew her to him, burying his face in the soft, scented hollows of her neck. She pressed her long, firm body against his.

'You're exhausted,' she said, with uncommon gentleness. 'Have you had a bad day?'

'Rotten. I'm not making any progress at all. At this rate Reg will be sending for the seventh cavalry.'

'I thought you'd got a gold star for catching the drug traffickers.'

'That was yesterday. Now he wants Frisco's murderer to round it off. Clean sweep to boast of next time the ACC rings up for a gossip. I'll just go and change, then I'll nip round and pick up Sophie.'

Alison followed him upstairs. 'You could just charge Penelope Swift with the murder and take the rest of your holiday,' she said provocatively.

'You silly girl,' Nick said with affection. 'Besides,' he added practically, 'the wretched woman turns out to have an unimpeachable alibi for Sunday evening. She was at the vicarage until gone one o'clock.'

'Whatever was she doing there until that hour?'

'Drinking his sherry and moaning about you, apparently.'

'It all sounds very dubious to me,' Alison said. 'Fake alibi, if ever I heard one.'

'It sounds only too plausible to me,' Nick replied, hanging his suit up carefully and slipping on a pair of jeans. 'Besides the vicar confirms it and vicars are fairly low down on my list of potential villains—providing they can keep their hands off the choir boys, of course.'

'Did you track down this "John" at the Dog and Duck?'

'That's how I know all the fates are conspiring against me,' Nick said peevishly. 'He turns out—predictably, I suppose—to be a long-distance lorry driver. He's disappeared to Marseilles for four days. He will find that Customs and Excise are more than usually interested in his load upon his return.'

'Marijuana?' Alison said. 'Is it worth bothering about? A lot of my friends—'

'Whoa! Stop,' Nick said. 'I don't want to hear. Anyway, the point is that he will be very quick to tell us what he knows about Alan Lawson and Frisco in exchange for lighter treatment on the hashish.'

'Things are bound to look up soon, my darling.'

Nick could see no logic behind such mindless optimism but he appreciated the thought and kissed her tenderly.

'Back in forty-five minutes.'

What passed for a rush hour in Hopbridge was long over and it was only twenty minutes later that Nick was pulling up outside the Armitages' house. Sophie was waiting for him. She had had her hair cut in Paris and looked, if anything, even plainer than before. He opened the passenger door for her and she got in.

'Isn't Alison's car lovely?' she said, with schoolgirl enthusiasm.

Nick laughed. 'I hate it.'

'Most men would give their eye teeth for a car like this.'

'That's another thing I hate about it.' He pulled out onto the Hopbridge road. 'The effect it has on other drivers. As soon as they see this car ahead of them a mad gleam comes into their eyes and they just have to overtake me—preferably on a blind corner.'

'What do they do when they see a woman at the wheel?'

'Huh, nobody overtakes Alison, not the speed she drives.'

After a short pause Sophie said bluntly, 'Mummy says that Alison won't marry you.' Nick smiled non-committally. He saw what Alison had meant about

Sophie. 'Mummy says she's a silly girl who doesn't know what's good for her,' she went on.

Nick laughed with genuine amusement. Sophie was really quite good value.

'Your mother is a very sensible woman. What a pity Alison never takes advice from anyone.'

'But why won't she?' Sophie persisted, with a puzzled frown.

'She gives a variety of reasons, some more acceptable than others.'

'For instance?'

'For instance, one: marriage is an out-moded idea; with which I do not agree. Two: that it would affect her tax position; which I can accept. Three: that we could not be happier than we are; which I am reluctantly obliged to concede. Perhaps she thinks I'm a gold digger.'

'I hadn't thought of that,' Sophie said seriously. Nick gave her an amused look. She flushed. 'That didn't come out quite right. All I meant was that it must be awkward, living with a woman who is so much richer than you are, in her house.'

'It could be awkward if we let it,' he agreed.

'But you don't?'

'If I told you how uninterested I was in Alison's money, you would never believe me, Sophie.'

'I don't know. I think I might.'

They passed through Hopbridge and swung on to the bridge, heading south towards Little Hopford.

'Oh, look,' Sophie said. 'There's the police station.' Nick admitted that he had noticed it before.

'I hadn't,' she said. 'And I must have been past it a thousand times.'

'I hope you never have cause to visit it, Sophie.'

'It must be very interesting, your job,' she ventured, with all the conviction of a linguaphone record.

'I can't think of anything I'd rather do, but ninety-nine per cent is frustrating routine. I've spent half the day looking for a man called John, who turns out to be a thousand miles away, and the other half looking for a man with a greyhound whom nobody knows. I'm beginning to think I hallucinated him.'

'You don't mean Salvatore, do you?' Sophie asked.

'What! You know him. You?'

'Guido Salvatore? He's a mine of information about the rise of fascism in Italy. I spent hours talking to him when I was researching my book on Mussolini last year.'

'So what does he look like, this Salvatore?'

'He must be over seventy now, tallish for an Italian—your height maybe—thin, and he has a greyhound bitch. Was it a bitch you were looking for?'

'I didn't get that well acquainted with the dog,' Nick said, in as serious a voice as he could muster. He didn't feel tired any more. He could almost see the dog squatting on the litter pile, not cocking its leg. A bitch. 'So where does this man live?'

'On the Freeman estate, a few miles across the moors. He was the odd job man there, ever since the war. Then when he retired they gave him a little cottage and a pension. He spends his time pottering about, walking the moors for hours. He's virtually a recluse.'

'He must speak English if he's been here since the war.'

'Not so's you'd notice. I had to communicate in a mixture of medieval Latin and pidgin English with sign language when all else failed. If you want to interrogate him—oh dear, what an awful word—question him, you may need an interpreter.'

'That's not the point. If he doesn't speak English he probably hasn't read the local papers.'

'I shouldn't think so for a moment. He always claims he doesn't like it here much: won't learn the language; hates the climate.'

'So why does he stay?'

'He was a prisoner of war here. I have a suspicion he knows so much about the fascist party because he was in it. I think after the war he was nervous to go back home in case there were people out to get him. So he stayed for a while and then it became a habit.'

'So he wouldn't send or receive letters,' Nick murmured to himself.

'I shouldn't think so.'

'No wonder no one knew who he was.'

Nick turned the car into the courtyard of Hope Cottage. The lights were on in the kitchen but the blinds were drawn.

'Seven-fifteen. Good, she'll still be listening to the *Archers* and won't hear the car.' He made a quick three-point-turn.

'The front door isn't locked, Sophie. Turn left inside and the kitchen is at the far end. Um, do you think you can break it to her gently that I've gone out again?'

TWENTY-TWO

SOPHIE APPEARED at the kitchen door. Alison switched the radio off, interrupting Peggy Archer in mid nag.

'Oh, leave it on!' Sophie said, catching the distant growl of the Jaguar. Alison took no notice.

'Won't be a minute, then we can go into the drawing room,' she said.

Outside blessed silence now reigned unchallenged. Sophie relaxed and perched on a stool. 'You are lucky, Alison.'

'Oh, do you like the house?'

'It's lovely, But I wasn't talking about that. I was talking about him: your lover-boyfriend-young-man. Wherever did you find him?'

'It's incredibly easy,' Alison told her. 'You arrange to have your cousin murdered practically in your back garden. You make sure you've got a good motive and no alibi. I guarantee a police inspector will be on your doorstep in no time. You might get a superintendent, if you're good.'

'But would he be a handsome, sensitive, intelligent police inspector?'

'Shh, he'll get a swollen head.'

'I don't think he can hear me.' Sophie fiddled nervously with a lemon on the worktop. She dropped it and knocked three jars of herbs over, trying to pick it up. Alison told her just to sit still and keep her hands in her lap.

'Where is the handsome inspector, anyway?' Alison asked. 'Gone to get you a drink, I trust.'

'Well, not exactly.'

NICK KNOCKED ON THE DOOR of the tiny stone cottage pointed out to him by one of the farm children. The door opened wide and he knew he had come to the right place.

'*Signor Salvatore? Questura.*' Nick showed the old man his warrant card.

Salvatore stood aside and motioned Nick in. The dog lumbered to its feet in token effort.

'Sit Beatrice,' Salvatore said, pronouncing the dog's name in the Italian fashion. 'She was never a very good guard dog and now she's older in dog years even than I am. But she likes to keep up the pretence. Pah! I've lived too long in this country, getting sentimental about animals now.' He switched on a lamp on the table and examined Nick. 'I've seen you before, often, on the moors.'

'That's right. Do you remember the last time you saw me?'

Salvatore scratched his head. 'Sit down, I'll make us some espresso.' He disappeared through a bead curtain into what was obviously the kitchen. Nick sat in an armchair in front of the empty grate. The greyhound came and laid her head on his foot. Nick scratched behind her ear and she gazed up at him in uncomplicated adoration. He didn't feel up to shouting questions about Frisco through the curtain.

Instead he said, 'Beatrice? Not Dante, surely?'

'Why not? She was young and beautiful once too, my Beatrice. Have you ever wondered what would have happened if Dante had married his Beatrice and she had grown old and fat?'

'He would have loved her still.' It sounded banal even to Nick. Funny the things you could come out with in another language. He was not surprised when the old man gave a cynical snort.

'You are not married, *Poliziotto*?'

'Not exactly.'

'Not exactly! Either you are married or you are not, there is nothing remotely like.'

'Not, then.'

'I thought not. If you want companionship, get a dog; sex, you can always buy, although the girls seem to give it away free these days.' He came back through the bead curtain with two tiny steaming cups.

'*E l'amore?*' Nick enquired mildly.

'*L'amore! Ingenuo!*'

He handed Nick one of the cups and Nick sipped the sweet, sticky liquid gratefully. He was beginning to feel hungry. Salvatore sat down opposite him.

'It can't have been less than two weeks ago,' he said. 'I've had bronchitis for the last two weeks. Haven't been out of the house. Bloody awful, damp climate!'

'You don't read the local papers?'

'No,' the old man said scornfully. 'I wouldn't read them if I could.'

Nick took the blurred school photo of Frisco out of his wallet. 'See her on the moors?'

'Oh yes, often. Lovely child. Never too busy to stop and speak to an old man, even one with an incomprehensible accent. So full of life.'

'She's dead,' Nick said quietly, wishing that he were not a policeman or that he was somewhere else. But Salvatore took the news philosophically.

'Ah! Nature has called her home.'

'No, it bloody hasn't! She was strangled up there, on Threeoaks Hill.'

'Threeoaks?' Salvatore got his tongue round the unfamiliar phonemes with difficulty.

'Where that little wood is.'

'Ah!' he said again. 'I begin to see the reason for your visit. I thought for a moment you had come to practise your excellent Italian on me.'

'Did you see her that afternoon, the day you last saw me?'

'Oh yes, not long before.'

'You walked to the copse from this direction, not from the valley?'

'Of course.'

'So you must have passed the lay-by on the moors road.' The old man leant back in his chair picturing the scene. 'There was a family car—I'm not very good at car makes—you know, a saloon car, with a family of trippers. They were picnicking out of the boot. And one of those little square French cars, like boxes on wheels.'

'What colour was it?' Nick asked, after he had digested the information.

'Yellow. Bright yellow.'

Nick drained his coffee cup and got up to go. The old man looked disappointed.

'Come again,' he said. 'When you can stay longer. I don't get many people to talk to.'

'Yes,' Nick said absently, his mind racing away. 'Yes, I will.'

'I SAW THE LAWSON BLOKE with her often these past few months,' Nick said aloud to himself. 'I saw the

Lorryson bloke with her often these past few months.
Christ! Oh, Meg. Poor Meg.'

HOPWOOD MANOR was in turmoil when Nick arrived
at half-past eight. There was no sign of Margaret in the
dining room. He found her eventually in the kitchen.

'Nick!' she said. 'I don't know which way to turn.'

'Where's Jean-Luc, Meg?'

'That's just it. He's gone. And the dining room full
again. I don't know how we're going to cope.'

Nick took her arm. 'We can't talk here. Let's go into
your office. I shall need to use the phone anyway.' She
stared at him wildly.

'I can't leave the kitchen.'

'You have any number of sous-chefs who have just
been waiting for this chance to show their prowess.
Come on, Meg.'

He led his cousin, protesting, into her office: an or-
derly, anonymous den.

'What time did he go?' Nick asked.

'About seven o'clock.'

'He hasn't got far then. Did he say where he was going?'

'Home, to the Pyrenees.'

'How did he go? In his car?'

'Yes.'

'What's the registration number?'

'I don't know.'

'What blood group is he?'

'I don't know.'

'Don't give me that! You got married in France, you
would have had blood tests at the time.'

'It was years ago. He's . . . group O. Stop barking
questions at me.'

Nick was sympathetic but firm. 'Sit down, Meg, you look worn out. I've got to ask a few things. Where do you keep the car documents?' He began to rummage through the neatly labelled files.

'In the car,' she said.

'What!'

'He always kept them in the car so we knew where they were.'

'Shit!'

'I'm sorry,' she said, close to tears.

'Come on, Meg,' Nick said kindly. 'Bear up.' He picked up the phone.

'It's no good,' she said hopelessly. 'You won't get him to come back.'

'I bloody well will. Be a darling and rustle up something to eat for me, I'm starving.' She left the office obediently as he got through to the station.

'No, I haven't got the registration, you'll have to manage without it. He should be easy enough to spot. Ring me if you find him, I don't care if it's four o'clock in the morning.' Nick gave them the number of Hope Cottage. 'The ports are the main thing. He hasn't had time to get out of the country yet. If he slips out now I shall have someone by the balls for it. OK?' He hung up.

Meg got back with some sort of cold pie. She slumped down on the chair again and began to cry. Nick opened the desk and found a small bottle of brandy in one of the cubby holes. He poured her a glass.

'Here. Drink this. What did he say before he left, Meg?'

'He's been so upset about Frisco.'

'You knew about him and her?'

'Not until tonight.'

'He told you, tonight?'

'It had been preying on his mind, ever since she was ... Then today he met Aunt Avis in town and she gave him a copy of the local paper, to show him the announcement of Lorna's engagement. There was a piece on the front page about the inquest. That was the first he knew of her being pregnant. That was the last straw. He told me the whole story and said that he'd made up his mind to contact the police, to go and see you. He trusted you to treat him fairly.'

'Why didn't he then?'

She looked at him defiantly. 'I told him not to trust *anyone*. I told him to go instead. To get away while there was still time. I thought he'd have longer. I don't know what's brought you here tonight—I didn't think you'd get on to him so quickly.'

Nick crouched down by her chair until their faces were level. 'Meg, my dear. Look at me. Did he confess to you that he'd killed her?'

Margaret hesitated then said, 'No. He didn't.'

LORNA CHASED OUT the regulars, including Constable Protheroe, at twenty to eleven. For once they left uncomplainingly. Lorna began to wash up. Her hands were bare for Dr Savage, who was an ambitious young man and didn't want a jailbird for a father-in-law and who, as fiancé, had enjoyed some of the privileges previously denied him, had asked for his ring back. Lorna had returned it without a word. Remembering that she had kept her dignity would console her, perhaps, during the long days and nights ahead.

Kit cleared the rest of the tables and began to help with the washing up.

'Not like you to make yourself useful,' Lorna grumbled.

'Someone's got to look after the place while Dad's away,' Kit said cheerfully. He looked older, the pinched look of discontent gone from his face. He put his arms round his sister and embraced her. He did it clumsily, holding her too tightly, since it was fifteen years since he had shown her any affection and he had forgotten how. Lorna appreciated the thought however and laid her head on his shoulder.

'Is it Dad?' he asked.

'Not really.'

'Edward?' She nodded. He patted her hair. 'You're a lovely girl, Lorna. You don't look anything like twenty-eight either. Everyone thinks you're my younger sister.'

'Only because I make a point of telling them so,' Lorna snivelled.

'There'll be another one along in a minute.'

'I don't want another one.' Lorna began to sob on her brother's shoulder.

'I wanted this one.'

IT WAS LATE when Nick reached Hope Cottage. He found Alison and Sophie in the drawing room.

'I'm sorry, my angel.'

'I'm not speaking to you,' Alison said.

'No? I shall have to talk to Sophie then. Sophie, I can't apologise enough. Whatever must you think of me?'

'I think you're lovely.'

'Shut up, Sophie,' Alison said, in disgust. 'He looks pleased enough with himself as it is.'

Nick shook his head slowly and sat down on the floor at Alison's feet. 'No. The case is breaking, but I don't like the look of the pieces.' He laid his head against her knee and she began to stroke his hair absent-mindedly.

'Did you find Salvatore?' Sophie asked. 'Was he any use?'

'Yes and yes. I now know the identity of Frisco's mystery lover.'

'Well, who was it?' Alison said impatiently. 'Don't keep us in suspense.'

'Thought you weren't talking to me.'

'Nick!' She pulled his hair.

'Ouch!' Nick thought for a moment. 'All right. You'll know soon enough. His picture will be in all the papers tomorrow, saying that we want to interview him.' He laughed unconvincingly. 'To "eliminate him from our enquiries". It was Jean-Luc.'

They were silent for a moment. Then Alison said, 'So you haven't arrested him.'

'No, he's done a bunk. We'll soon catch him.'

'What happens?' Sophie asked. 'Do you have all your men out looking for him?'

'Not quite. Every policeman in the country now has his description and that of his car. Our best chance is when he tries to leave the country. Sweetheart, I know it's a stupid question, but you don't happen to know the registration number of Jean-Luc's car, do you?'

'No, no idea. Can't you find out? From some police computer.'

'No, I can find out a name and address from a number but not vice versa.'

LATER THAT NIGHT Nick said, 'I got the impression I didn't have your full attention then, Al.'

'Don't call me Al. I was thinking.'

'So much for my devastating sexual technique.'

'Margaret and Jean-Luc bought their cars at the same time, last autumn.'

'Yes, I remember.'

'From the Renault dealer in Taunton.'

'Yes, so?'

'Haven't you ever bought a new car?'

'No.'

'They have a range of registration numbers allocated to them,' she explained patiently. 'When you buy a new car they allocate you the next one on the list, or they ask you to choose one. The two cars would have adjacent numbers, or very nearly. Where the hell are you going?'

'Up to Hopwood, obviously. I can hardly call Margaret at half-past one in the morning and ask her what the number of her car is. She'll be asleep.'

'Wish I was,' Alison grumbled. She lay back against the pillow and thought some more. When Nick got back forty minutes later she had thought the whole thing through, and was asleep.

TWENTY-THREE

'HE WON'T GET FAR,' Nick said the next morning. 'They've got most of the car number now. He'll be picked up by midday for sure. What's the matter, my angel?'

'You're assuming he's still alive, Nick?'

'Of course. What do you mean? Suicide? I suppose it's possible.'

'No,' she said gently. 'I don't mean suicide. Has it occurred to you to ask why Jean-Luc should kill Frisco?'

'Well... she was pregnant. I suppose she told him that night and he just panicked.'

'Jean-Luc loved children. It was the great sorrow of his life that he and Margaret couldn't have any.'

'Wherever did you get that idea?' Nick said, in amazement.'

'From Avis, I suppose,' she admitted. 'But it's true, Nick. Margaret once said something to me which confirmed it. Men don't hear these things. Women talk about them only when the men aren't around.'

'It's not as if you and she were exactly close,' Nick said stiffly. 'Why should she talk to you about it?'

'Women do. They tell things to quite casual girl-friends they would never dream of discussing with their husbands or brothers. It's true.'

'So what are you saying?'

'That Jean-Luc would have been delirious with joy when he found out that Frisco was pregnant. She said herself he would be delighted. Killing her would have been the last thing on his mind.'

'So she told him it wasn't his. Destroyed all his happiness with one blow.'

'She told Alan Lawson that she had met someone she could be happy with. Alan assumed she meant Ben and so did you but I told you all along that she had no intention of marrying Ben—she was just winding Dot up. She was talking about Jean-Luc.'

'But if he didn't kill her, why has he done a bunk now?'

Alison shook her head. 'I hope you're right, Nick. Truly I do.'

THE PHONE RANG early that evening. Nick answered.

'They've got him,' he said as he hung up. 'Trying to get the Roscoff boat at Plymouth. They're sending him back. I'll get off straight away.'

Alison followed him out to the car. 'Will you promise me something, Nick?'

'What?'

'Come home afterwards. Here.'

'Well, of course I will,' he said in astonishment. 'Why shouldn't I? I may be very late though.'

'Just promise me however late it is; however bad you feel, you'll come home.'

'I promise,' he said, puzzled.

'I love you, Nick,' Alison called after the car, but the noise from the faulty engine drowned her voice and Nick did not hear her.

BILL DEACON was not a happy man.

'It might be best if you stayed here, sir.'

'No, I'll come with you.'

'Please, sir.'

'I'm coming, I said.'

'Yes, sir. How many constables should we take?'

'Good God, man,' Nick said, in disgust, 'She's not dangerous.'

THEY REACHED Hopwood Manor at midnight. They found Margaret in the kitchen. She seemed to be expecting them.

'Hello, Nick,' she said, removing her apron and stuffing it in the laundry basket. 'I thought Jean wouldn't get very far. Not with his appearance and accent.'

Bill looked nervously round the room, taking in the great steel knives of which there seemed to be hundreds. Nick felt him shift his weight on to the balls of his feet, ready to spring if necessary.

'Are you coming then, Meg?' he said gently.

'Just let me get my coat, from the house.'

'We'll come with you.' Nick nodded to Bill who laid a hand on her arm and arrested her.

I AM Margaret Lohitzun-Mendi, restaurateur, of Hopwood Manor. I am writing this statement in the presence of Detective Inspector Trevellyan and Detective Sergeant Deacon. I make this statement of my own free will. I understand that I need not say anything unless I wish to do so and that what I say may be given in evidence. I strangled Frisco Carstairs and I wish to state how this came about.

I knew that my husband had been having an affair with Frisco. He didn't know I knew. I turned a blind eye to it. I knew Frisco and thought that she would soon grow tired of him or find someone else. I didn't

tackle him about it as I didn't want to force a show-
down. I was so afraid of losing him.

My husband came from a large family and was very
fond of children. For several years after our marriage
we tried to have children but weren't able to. We had
some tests done and I was the one at fault. Oh, they
don't put it quite like that, of course, "It's no one's
fault, dear, just one of those things." Patronising bas-
tards! I even had an operation but it made no difference. Jean-Luc was bitterly disappointed but he came
to accept it over the years and never reproached me for
it.

On the day Frisco died my aunt, Avis Trevellyan,
came to lunch at the manor. She is the receptionist at
the Health Centre in Hopbridge and the worst gossip
in the valley. She didn't know about Jean's affair with
Frisco as I would never have confided in her. So it was
in a spirit of pure gossip that she told me that Frisco
Carstairs was pregnant. She had been into the Health
Centre for a test and the results had come back on the
Saturday. Frisco hadn't even had them yet.

I tried to tell myself that the child was not necessarily Jean's—that any one of a number of men could
have fathered it. I didn't know then about her supposed engagement to Ben Lawson. I tried to reason
with myself but my heart told me that it was Jean's. I
still think that it was. I was frantic, not knowing what
he would do when he found out. I couldn't bear to lose
him, you see.

We're not open on Sunday night so Jean often went
off to meet her then as well as in the afternoons. That
night I said I was going out to the cinema in Minehead
and would be back late. I waited around until I saw
Jean drive off. I knew they had started meeting on

Threeoaks Hill since the weather had improved. He took the moors road, as he usually did, leaving his car in the lay-by. I drove down the valley to Great Hopford and walked up. It's quite a walk and they had finished by the time I got there.

I waited until Jean had gone and then I approached her. I'm not sure why, wanting to reason with her perhaps—ask her to let me and Jean have the baby. I switched on my torch. She couldn't see me, of course, she would have been dazzled. She was sitting there leaning up against a tree, her skirt still round her thighs. She gave one of those smiles of hers and said 'John, is that you?' I lost all reason. She was wearing some sort of tawdry scarf round her neck. I grabbed it and pulled. She was much smaller than me, thin—like a child—she didn't put up much fight. When I came to my senses, she was dead. I was appalled. I'd killed her. I'd killed Jean's child. I just ran away as fast as I could.

When Jean heard she was dead he just sort of retreated into himself. I don't know how I kept going. I haven't slept a wink since that night. Then Jean saw the report of the inquest in the paper and found out she had been pregnant. Yesterday evening he said that he was going to the police to tell them about her and him. So I told him what I had done, I just couldn't stand it any more. I'm glad it's all come out. I couldn't live with myself any longer.

He didn't say much, just that if he stayed he'd be sure to give me away. He packed a few things and set off, home. My actions had lost him more surely than by anything Frisco could have done. I didn't mean to kill her. I just couldn't bear to lose him.

'SHE'S SIGNED the statement and been charged, sir,' Bill
said. 'I think you ought to go home. Let me drive you.'

'Drive me?' Nick said vaguely. 'It's just round the
corner.'

Bill looked at him with concern, then patted his
shoulder.

'Hope Cottage, Nick. Don't you want to go home to
Hope Cottage?'

'Oh. Yes. I must. I promised.'

'Miss Hope will take care of you.'

'OK.' Nick no longer felt capable of making deci-
sions. He allowed Bill to help him into his coat and
followed him obediently out to the car park.

IT WAS HALF-PAST ONE when Bill delivered Nick home.
Alison was not in bed and was at the front door by the
time they got there. Nick walked past her in a daze.

'What happened?' Alison asked Bill.

'We arrested Mrs Lorryson-Monday, Miss...Alison.
He's taken it very hard.'

'Thanks for bringing him home, Bill.'

'It was the least I could do. Goodnight. Goodnight,
sir. Miss Alison will take good care of you.' Bill looked
at Alison for a moment, wondering if she was up to the
job. Nick did not reply but stood, staring round the hall
as if unsure where he was. Then he went into the
drawing room. Bill watched him go with concern.

'I could...stay for a bit, if you thought it would
help,' he said awkwardly. Alison wanted to kiss him for
caring so much but she feared it would just embarrass
him. She squeezed his arm instead.

'You get home, Bill. You're exhausted.'

'Shake him out of it,' Bill said. 'Don't let him wal-
low in it. That's the worst thing.' Their eyes met and he

realised suddenly that she *was* up to the job—that
nothing Nick could ask of her would be too much for
her. He smiled and nodded, relieved.

'Goodnight, Alison.' On impulse he stepped forward and kissed her on the cheek. Then he blushed
scarlet and turned briskly away. He got back into his
car and drove off. Alison followed Nick into the drawing room where he was sitting on the floor in front of
the dead grate, his head buried in his knees.

'Have you eaten? Shall I get you something?' she
asked.

He shook his head dumbly.

'Drink? Some brandy? I know you don't normally
but it might do you good, just this once.'

No reply.

She sat down on the floor, close to him but not
touching, wondering how to reach him. She tried
again.

'It's me, Alison,' she said. 'Talk to me, Nick, my
dearest love. Don't freeze me out like this—I can't bear
it. Don't do this to us. Let me help.'

At last he raised his head and looked at her. 'You
knew,' he said accusingly.

'I didn't *know* anything. Guessed perhaps. I thought
it more likely Margaret than Jean-Luc.'

'Why didn't you say?' he demanded angrily. 'Why
didn't you prepare me for it at least? Why did you let
me walk in there with my eyes closed?'

'Because I hoped to God that I was wrong.'

'That's why you made me promise to come home.'

'I know what you're like when you're unhappy. You
just let it eat away at you instead of talking about it. I
had no idea you would take it this hard, though. I
know you were fond of her—'

'I loved her,' he corrected. 'Still love her.'

'You weren't like this when you arrested Lynton.'

'Lynton did what he did deliberately and callously—he deserved to be punished. Anyway, it's not that exactly. Perhaps I will have that brandy.'

Alison fetched the bottle and poured them both a glass. She sat down again a little closer to him. He sipped the brandy and made a face.

'It tastes foul,' he said belligerently. 'How can you drink this stuff for pleasure? ... Why did you think Jean-Luc might be dead?'

'I wasn't sure of the state of her mind. I thought if he had found out—turned from her in disgust, maybe—she might have killed him. Perhaps herself too. Thank God I was wrong. Will she stand trial for murder?'

'Almost certainly. That's what she's been charged with. She may get off with a plea of manslaughter.'

'What will happen to her?'

Nick made a helpless gesture. 'It could be anything. If she's found guilty of murder it will be life. If the jury accepts manslaughter with diminished responsibility she could be out in a few years. Either way, her life is over. She has lost the one thing she cared about.'

'Jean-Luc? What will happen to him?'

'He'll go home to the Basque country, I think. We won't hold him. We can't force him to give evidence against her and I don't think he will do it voluntarily. He loved her too.'

'It hardly seems possible, does it? A crime of passion.'

He glared at her suddenly and his voice rose in anger. 'Because they're both so plain and stolid, you mean? Love is reserved for the young and beautiful, is it? Women like Meg suffer all the more when it goes wrong. She kept saying over and over, "I couldn't bear to lose him, you see". It cut me to the heart. I kept asking myself what I would have done in her position—if I thought I was going to lose you. Is it worth all the uncertainty? All the heartache?'

'Yes, my darling. It is. And you are not like Margaret.'

He put the full glass of brandy down on the hearth and got up. He ran his hands through his already dishevelled hair and looked down at her.

'When you had lunch with Lucy, the other day, did she tell you why we split? She and I?'

'No. I told you, we didn't really talk about you.'

'She left me because she loved me.'

'I don't understand.'

'She loved me and I didn't love her. So she left me. She said it would be less painful in the long term. I didn't understand either, not at the time.'

'I don't understand it now,' Alison whispered. 'It sounds insane to me.' She stared up at him in desperation.

'I'm beginning to understand what she meant,' he said calmly. 'They say that in any relationship there is one who loves and one who allows herself to be loved—one who kisses and one who offers the cheek. That's how it has been with us, Alison.'

'No! . . . No!'

'I've never made any secret of my feelings for you—I don't suppose I could have, even if I'd wanted to. But you...there've been times I thought all you wanted was a tame poodle. By your fireside. In your bed.'

'I love you like crazy, Nick.'

'Perhaps it's too late for that, Alison. I'm not sure I believe you.'

'I love you. Dear God! What do you want me to say? I love your strange sense of humour and your tolerance and your kindness and your stupid hair which won't stay in place for five minutes and your *integrity* and your sarcasm and your lovely, skinny body which always knows exactly how to please mine. I love you.'

'Then why the hell couldn't you have said so in the first place like any normal woman?'

'I was afraid.'

'Afraid of what, for Christ's sake? Of me?'

'No, of course not. Of myself. Of my own feelings. Of being hurt. Of giving you the power to hurt me. Of being ... *crushed* by a more dominant personality.'

'Crushed? You? Don't make me laugh, Alison.'

'You don't know your own strength, Nick.'

'I can't talk about it now. I don't know what I want any more.' He walked away from her. 'I'm worn out. I'll sleep in the spare room. I can't think about it to-night.'

'No, you won't sleep in the spare room,' she screamed, running after him into the hall. 'You bloody well will think about it tonight. I love you and I won't let you go. Do you hear?'

She seized him by the arm and forced him to turn back. He had long ago concluded that she was incapable of tears and now he stared in astonishment at her wet cheeks. His anger melted away and he took her in his arms, the woman he had waited for all his life, and kissed the tears away.

'I've made you cry,' he said penitently. 'I never thought I'd see proud, tough Alison Hope in tears.'

She buried her face in his shoulder, her body racked with sobs.

'Things will have to be different from now on, Alison.'

Author of *Mom Doth Murder Sleep* and
Mom Meets Her Maker

First
Time in
Paperback

MOM AMONG THE LIARS
JAMES YAFFE

STRANGE BEDFELLOWS

Everybody talks under the influence of Mom's chicken potpie—
especially her son, Dave, an investigator with the public
defender's office in Mesa Grande, Colorado. Discussing
cases with Mom has become routine—her logic and rattrap
brain have helped him solve many murders.

Amid the heat of a tight political race, Edna Pulaski, a local
madam, is murdered. The prime suspect is a homeless derelict.
The case seems open-and-shut, and the district attorney, who is
up for reelection, wants a fast conviction. But Mom's got a nose
for exactly the kind of hanky-panky going on in Mesa Grande's
corridors of power. So does the killer.

"A lively and entertaining mystery..."   —*Publishers Weekly*

Available in April at your favorite retail stores.

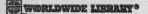

Where do you find hot Texas nights, smooth Texas charm and dangerously sexy cowboys?

Crystal Creek reverberates with the exciting rhythm of Texas. Each story features the rugged individuals who live and love in the Lone Star State.

"...Crystal Creek wonderfully evokes the hot days and steamy nights of a small Texas community...impossible to put down until the last page is turned."
—*Romantic Times*

"...a series that should hook any romance reader. Outstanding."
—*Rendezvous*

Praise for Bethany Campbell's *The Thunder Rolls*

"Bethany Campbell takes the reader into the minds of her characters so surely...one of the best Crystal Creek books so far. It will be hard to top...."

Don't miss the next book in this exciting series. Look for RHINESTONE COWBOY by BETHANY CAMPBELL

Available in May wherever Harlequin books are sold.

A FINE ITALIAN HAND

First Time in Paperback

Eric Wright

An Inspector Charlie Salter Mystery

CHECKOUT TIME

Murder at the seedy Days 'R Done motel is no surprise. But the killing of actor Alec Hunter poses some questions for Toronto Police Inspector Charlie Salter. Namely, what was a nice guy like Alec doing in a place like that?

His death appears to be the work of a fine Italian hand—a Mob-style hit—carried out to settle some gambling debts. Yet the Mob denies the charges. So who was the Italian-looking gentleman who registered for Alec's room at the Days 'R Done?

"Excellent series...humor and insight."

—*New York Times Book Review*

Available in May at your favorite retail stores.

Author of *Larkspur*

Sheila Simonson

SKYLARK

A Lark Dodge Mystery

First Time in Paperback

CULTURE SHOCK

When San Francisco bookstore owner Lark Dodge and her friend Ann rent a flat in London, they anticipate a bit of bookseller's business and a lot of touristy fun. They get murder.

A new acquaintance, a Czech poet, is stabbed on the tube, and Lark makes a quick copy of a valuable manuscript he'd handed her before turning the original over to the police. Perhaps that explains the ransacking of her flat. But what about the brutal murder of her stuffy landlady and her beloved pooch?

"Self-aware and intelligent, the clearly drawn Lark is a promising new presence on the mystery scene."
—*Publishers Weekly*

Available in June at your favorite retail stores.

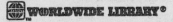 **WORLDWIDE LIBRARY®**

SKYLARK

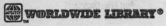